Acknowledgements

An earlier version of *Up On the Roof* was published in *Noon, Stories and Poems from Sosltice Shorts Festival 2018*, Arachne Press, 2019
An earlier version of *The Greenhouse* was published in The Newcastle University Anthology for Creative Writing Students, 2019

D1493728

Accidental Flowers

Contents

Beginning

Middle

Ending

After

Beginning

2030

Bliss

Everyone says that they love spring because of the longer days and the green leaves, but I think the real reason that people love spring is because of cow parsley. Would that I could sell the bliss that cow parsley brings. *Anthriscus sylvestris* – a silvery cloudy line that links cities to the countryside, seaside towns to landlocked hamlets. Heaven in a plant.

It's May and muggy with it. I have made it through the traffic in the city, a slow process, accompanied by the sound of too-loud talk radio, and rumbling from other road users. I'm now heading out into the country. My SatNav tells me I have twenty or so glorious minutes of winding sixty mph roads, bordered by happy banks of – yes, you guessed it – cow parsley.

Freedom.

If I were to marry, I'd do it in May. I can see it all: jugs of cow parsley spilling onto tables, cow parsley buttonholes, cow parsley accessories for my hair, letting all the indigent creatures crawl from the stems and build a home on my scalp.

*

Bliss and I met in May. A long time ago, at a party. We were both fifteen and it was one of those house parties that started off with bowls of Doritos and ended with local boys coming around to smash televisions and pull chests of drawers apart. Their arrival signalled that it was time to leave (if you hadn't already left with your latest crush, of course).

We were standing in the narrow, noisy kitchen. Some of the skinny girls, the ones from our year or the year below, the ones who still looked like infants, were sat cross-legged on counter-tops.

I'd offered Bliss a drink from my can of cider. She'd declined. She didn't drink, not then.

'It messes with my artistic nature,' she informed me, her eyes lost beneath a thick layer of shimmering blue makeup. I fell in love.

*

Apart from the occasional surprising Land Rover, the roads are quiet. Cows stand pressed against the hedge, their big black snouts poking through the hedgerows. I want to put my hand out of the window and boop their noses, but I'm going too fast. And cows have always scared me. It is the city girl in me perhaps, I'm wary of their sheer size. The SatNav beeps a speed warning. I take my foot from the pedal as the road hairpins. Something I've not secured well enough hits the side of the truck with a metallic ping. Possibly the watering can? Possibly the handle of a now ruined tool?

It always surprises me how well gardening businesses do in May. I mean, the best time to plan a summer garden is actually in October, but it's the cow parsley thing again. People live on scrubland all year around and then they take one May walk through the park and there grows inside them this aching desire for a perfect, bee-humming, paradise-possessing back yard. Before last year, I was always so busy in April and May. So busy, that when I shut my eyes, all I saw were the fine veins on the surface of a leaf, or the curl of an unfurling bulb. So busy, especially if it was warm.

And when isn't it warm now?

*

Our friendship was never equal. Our loyalty to each other was fierce, but, at any one time, one of us always loved the other more. Her addiction to the melodramatic gave me a stomach ache and she thought I liked boys too much, that I spent too much time pining. Her eyes would roll when I said I was in love with a boy, but when she fell for 'the one', it was the end of the world if (when) he didn't call her back. My school was 'too posh' for her, and I hated the way she would act as if her school was situated in a war zone, and that going to it was equal to risking her life.

I grew up on the sort of road where everyone's hedge was big enough and wide enough to hide their goings-on. She and her mum shared a garden with their upstairs neighbours. A garden with an apricot tree and courgettes, with their pretty yellow flowers that Bliss's mum would batter for us if we asked enough times.

If Bliss's clothes were loose on me, she would throw a tantrum. If her feet were slight enough to wear a pair of ridiculous heels I couldn't get past my little toes, I refused to talk to her for a week.

But really, for two wistful teenage girls, we were equally vital to the other. We grew up and, unaware, we became tangled, like two French dwarf bean seedlings, left to their own devices on a sunny windowsill.

*

There are hearty helpings of apple blossom here and there en route – ornamental orchards, there for show rather than produce. My mental boundaries blur and although I am currently on a winding country road and in complete control of the van, in my mind I'm elsewhere – on her hospital ward, by her bedside. Her cheeks are as pink as apple blossom, the rest of her skin the pale brown of new bark. Her lips still tinged green, the colour of new leaves.

I can remember how helpless she looked. I can still see the police on their way down the corridor. Even on this beautiful spring day, the birds competing with the engine, I am still shaken to the core.

*

We grew apart, letting our shoots aim towards different patches of sunlight. It was such a slow process that there was no dawning realisation, no sudden devastation. Just a sporadic pang of loss, occasionally brought on by a change in the weather, like the sudden drip of a pipe reminding you that you meant to fix it last autumn, before the rain.

By the time we reconnected, Bliss had made a lot more of herself than I had. Don't get me wrong, I loved my job. Running my own small garden design business allowed me to pass my weeks in the quiet friendship of plants and fertiliser, spades and seedlings. I was paid to spend other people's money on wrought iron furniture and decorative pebbles. It was a gift, to be rewarded for merely observing and occasionally facilitating, green, earthy life. I became fit and slight and quick-fingered.

But Bliss, Bliss had actually become famous. She was a celebrity. She had rendered into reality the dreams we used to discuss over a box of chips, the night bus home taking its sweet, slow time.

When I first saw her face on the advertisement on the side of a bus, I was on a date, sitting in a pub garden. Lime fizzed in my tonic, bubbles popped on their pint. Bliss had done it! She had a leading role! As the vehicle sped past us and on up the high street, I had lifted my drink in stone-cold admiration for my old friend, and said 'to Bliss'. Upon reflection, I think I may have instilled some false hope in the acquaintance opposite me, who, incidentally, I didn't meet up with again.

*

By taking in gulps of the sweet smelling, almost alcoholic air hammering through the window, I manage to bring myself back to the present. I am speeding again. My shoulders have levered themselves up to my ears and my back aches as I force them back down. I slow as I come to a crossroads. The SatNav tells me straight on, but the signs say differently.

To the future, says the one to the left. I'm not ready, am I?

To regret, says the one on the right. Not again.

I put my foot down and screech across, following the sign that says *head down, but chin up*.

*

Dear Ms Forrest,

– went the emailed request –

You may not remember me, but I remember you. We grew up together, shared mutual friends. Your mum told mine that you had started a garden business and that your work was, as your mum put it, 'exquisite'.

– Sounds like mum, always in my corner. Or on my side of the courtroom.

I've just moved out of the city and finally have a yard,

– interesting choice of word for what turned out to be a huge oasis of horticultural potential.

and we haven't a clue what to do with it. Would we be able to book you in for as long as it takes to fix it?

– it took a lot longer to fix than either of us expected, didn't it Bliss?

*

Before the court case, when I was driving to visit a new client, I would try to imagine what they looked like, how they behaved. My ruminations were always biased. Even now, my first impressions of people are fully formed before I even meet them. It is all down to how they contact me. If they email, then I respect their professional nature, their desire to keep everything above board – to have a 'paper' trail. If they text me, I know that they're either single parents with very little time or looking at their patches of land like it is a second thought. So, it was lovely, driving out to Bliss's new 'yard', the anticipation of our reunion bubbling in my stomach like water moving through dried-out soil. For the business, this deal was huge. I had never considered that kind of money or the demand of creativity. It was a job that should have set me up for life, but the legal fees devoured most of it like a snail on a marigold.

For me, the deal was about far more than money.

And her face, when I saw it, was just as lovely as portrayed on the many screens on which I'd watched her. A few more marks of life, but as delicate and supple as it always had been.

She had opened the door with a gin and tonic in a coupe. A few peels of grapefruit sailed across the top, a tonic-induced tang jumping to my top lip when she went in for the hug I had hoped for. It was just after lunch, but she was hazy with day-drinking. A floral silk shirt hung about her brown body. She was a magnolia incarnate.

I fell in love all over again.

*

That day, as the size of the project became clearer, we talked business. We knew there would be time enough for the rest, time for the roots of our friendship to begin to show again, shivering and tender, peeking above a decade of soil. She kept trying to press a cocktail on me, I kept nodding back to my van, *Forrest Horticulture* emblazoned across the back doors in teal lettering. Keeping my business close, as an excuse.

She was wonderfully haughty, like she had always wanted to be. She spoke over me constantly, as she always had. She wanted a vegetable patch, a pond, two separate seating areas, bamboo and flowering shrubs, ornamental trees and fruiting shrubs, grasses and variegated shrubs and...

'Everything.' She drained her glass, looking at me from her above her over-large sunglasses. 'Can you give me everything?'

*

I have to pull over. I am finding it hard to breathe. All my fault. I plead guilty – guilty for taking the road down memory lane. A journey bordered by edible flowers in a golden batter and the bunches of cow parsley and earth-dribbling daisy chains strung in my hair by Bliss's teenage fingers while we dozed in the sun of my back garden. I have let the doubts move about, and now I must wait for them to settle, to drop, to decompose.

*

It took me a year, along with my team, to complete it all. We were so wrapped up in it that we had to work through the torrential summer rain, to work hard to stop the bulbs coming up too early in the unusual December warmth of that year. Bliss was around occasionally, but nowhere near as much as I would have liked. Whoever hired her would pay to fly her out to thrillingly exotic locations, where plants grew of such size and beauty that I could only dream. Even when flying became more difficult, what with the bans on certain countries within the EU, and the stricter rules on carbon emissions; somehow, she still managed to travel.

When she did return from filming, or tours, she would make me walk around the plot and tell her everything that I had done, show her every single thing I had planted, and explain it all. Her need for knowledge was almost as voracious as her thirst for the white wine she cupped in one slender hand. I didn't care. I was so proud of the borders and the colours and the way everything, once settled, looked like an image from the sorts of gardening magazines my parents used to read on the toilet. I was proud of my entrepreneurial research, of the different seeds I had ordered from the other side of the world (it was easier then to buy produce from Australia than it was Spain), so chuffed to be able to tell her that her vegetable patch was as original as she was.

Like I said at the trial: my desire for her affections almost killed her.

She always made me stay for dinner and, if she managed to get me drunk enough, for the night. We would lie in her huge bed in her huge room and giggle through memories that had been made between then and now. We would fall asleep against the stacked pillows, our heads bobbing in our snores like fuchsias on the wind.

*

This is the first business request we've had since my name was cleared. The first person who has looked below the tabloid line and seen the potential that their back/front/side garden has to offer. It must be the warmer weather, the ever-tightening environmental restrictions on flying – people want more from their outside spaces, or maybe this person just doesn't know who I am yet. Maybe they'll see my face and I'll look familiar and they'll Google me and that will be that.

The SatNav says two minutes to go. I'm on my way now, aren't I?

*

When they took her into the hospital, no one knew what was wrong. There are still quite a lot of unknowns surrounding her illness, especially as she was the first one in the UK (that we know of) to have been affected. According to the trial, they pumped her stomach at the scene – but only because the shattered glass around her prone body made them think she had drunk too much. It was a blessing that they did. Emptied her out, right there and then, on her almost-new morning patio.

It was then that they brought up the slimy, black, half-digested aubergine from her stomach. It was then that they dug through her records, through her potting shed (also painted teal, to remind her of me), through the tins and boxes I had organised in neat, alphabetically-labelled fashion.

It was then that they found a selection of the seed packets I had ordered from abroad. The ones that would be used as evidence in the trial of R v Forrest.

It was then that I got the phone call.

*

I start the engine, pull back onto the road. No one has passed me, but I look around me anyway. It is clouding over, as it always does at this time of day. With the gulf stream breaking down, the erratic behaviour of the weather is becoming increasingly predictable. I hope that the customer will offer me a cup of tea, because I need the sugar. I am a bee, losing its buzz.

My hands stick to the steering wheel.

*

According to Doctor Williams, the scientist who supported me in the trial, it wasn't just the seeds. She was so young, but she knew so much. She hated the limelight, but loved the research part. She told me – and the jury – that the seeds wouldn't have turned to poison if the soil hadn't been infected. After the trial, she told me – and my mum – that what had happened was a good thing in the long run. That it will teach us all something about our world. She asked if I would be a case study for part of her research that she was conducting for the Committee for Climate Change, all about the impending crisis.

According to Doctor Williams, Bliss will not be the only one to suffer such a fate.

*

I pull into the driveway of a wisteria-lined cottage. It has begun to rain, but one of the sash windows is still wide open – the heat hasn't dissipated. I park and unstick myself from the seat. The plant arching across the wall is an old-timer.

13

There is comfort in that: the soil is still giving it what it needs, and vice versa.

*

Bliss will come out of hospital, eventually. Her mum updates my mum, which is kind. Bliss never really thought I'd tried to poison her, but her people took hold of the wrong end of the stick and that was that.

Technically, I am culpable.

When she does emerge, blinking in the bright, constant light, she'll see they've overturned her vegetable patch, cordoned it off. She'll read about all the new laws and regulations that have been put in place because of my bad luck. She'll see how those days of eating apricots straight from the tree are gone.

It is all different now.

*

Or is it? I turn away from the cottage and look back the way I drove in. The hedges are fluttered with cow parsley, holding petals to the rain in gleeful acceptance. They don't bend, or break. They don't give in. They bed down, shoot up.

See? You can't help but smile.

All Bosom and Pride

Joanna could see the face of the young woman beside her in the reflection of her phone. It looked unwieldy and not ideal for a day of rebellion. The reflection was somewhat disgruntled. Joanna always thought that a furrowed brow on a young face made it seem even younger. When Martha's frons knitted together, it took Joanna right back to bath-time, to car journeys in the baby seat, to rushed and squashed picnics in the park. She must check her own phone soon, Martha had promised to text her the test results.

Joanna's breast swelled as she bellowed out her favourite of today's sayings: 'THERE IS NO PLANET B!', shocking the young woman in front of her into parcelling away her mobile and shaking her placard (how many hands did she have?). They looked sideways, flashed each other a grin.

'I'm Joanna.'

'Megan.'

They nodded in recognition of the companionship surrounding them, the hope that was at once fleeting and as sticky as the glue some of their comrades would later use to adhere themselves to an important pavement.

The crowd pushed slowly forward, a sea of sustainable raincoats ranging from sun yellow to hot pink, which clashed terribly with the burning rainforests and the cruel beige droughts decorating the placards of their owners.

Megan could feel her phone buzzing away in her pocket, but tried to ignore it. Her mum would not have been impressed.

'Taking selfies? On an important day like this?' Gathering one of her patterned shawls around her, all bosom and pride. 'Keep your chin up, Meg!' One smooth, clever hand raising her daughter's chin. 'This is a key moment in our history as humans!'

Ben nudged her, and with his voice full of the cold, sunny day and the excitement of people around him, shouted, 'Your mum would have loved this!'

Megan shrugged. Her mum would not have loved the news coming from Greenland, about the shattering ice caps, nor the government's reneging on the Paris Agreement. No net-zero by 2050, like they had promised.

For a split second, she imagined the woman beside her was her mum. Ben, seeing her eyebrows crinkle, shouted into the crowd on a stream of steam:

'ITS GETTING HOT IN HERE, SO TAKE OFF ALL YOUR COALS.'

It had the desired effect. Megan's face melted into a smile.

'Very clever,' nodded Joanna.

'Excuse me,' somebody (somebodies?) shunted into the back of Joanna. 'We need to get through.'

*

The old woman was moving so slowly, that it was beginning to annoy Nesta, whose sticky-handed children were making progress difficult. The sandwich board around her neck continually banged her knees, but she refused to let this impede her pursuit of justice.

'Come on you two! Remember what I told you – NOT OUR FUTURE, NOT OUR FUTURE!'

Their thin, six- and eight-year-old voices rang in unison. Nesta continued to charge forward, her *Solidarity With Our Planet* sign whacking into others as well as herself.

Typical, Joanna thought, bending and unbending her offended elbow. 'Me first, me first'. Having marched for decades (she, her husband and their friends had won the cold war, after all) Joanna knew how to keep her place in a throng. She made herself as wide as possible. She linked an arm into Megan's, who squeezed it against her, looking at Joanna with a wink. Joanna admired the wool of Megan's coat. Very soft, a beautiful colour. There were some fashions Joanna wished she could still wear. She had been the sort of young woman who was brave enough to wear teal. Martha should wear brighter colours, do away with those stylish yet boring business suits. Joanna had once questioned Martha's taste and had almost lost her head (and heart) in the fierce, and yet rather sad, chomp of her retort: 'Mum! Stop! We can't all be ageing hippies!'

Joanna wondered if Megan, this daughter-aged woman beside her, was part of a career path that demanded she hide her roots? As a little one, Martha used to roll around with bare limbs all summer long, throwing pudgy arms around tree trunks and tumbling down hillsides. Now, she worked for the petrol giants, her sharp heels splicing themselves into the Earth's core and slurping.

What had Joanna been marching for, these past thirty years?

Nesta's sigh was audible above the cheers, the whistles, the chants. She so desperately wanted to break through, to be at the front, to shake off the clammy clutches of her hard-won children. She wondered if Laura was here, like she'd promised. Now that was a soft, wedding-band-free hand she would happily clutch.

'I'm sorry,' she tried again, appealing to the younger woman. 'I'm trying to find someone at the front of the march.'

'But that's at least a mile ahead,' the older woman dismissed, her short silver hair bobbing with self-importance, or very expensive conditioner.

The young girl looked at her, a sympathetic twist on her brow. 'If you need company, you can march with us.' She glanced down at Nesta's youngest,

Elizabeth (Bert, for short) and gave her a wink. Bert grinned shyly back, wanting desperately for the nice lady to wink at her again.

With Mitchell a dead-weight pulling on Nesta's arm, staring up at the buildings towering above them, his nose running freely into his scarf, she was glad to relinquish a thrilled Bert to Megan, who put a bright-gloved arm on her shoulder and explained to her the latest chant: THE SEAS ARE RISING AND SO ARE WE!

Joanna glanced at the little boy, his cheeks pink with an incoming tantrum. He saw her looking and wiped his nose with his sleeve.

'Do you come on a lot of marches?' Joanna asked, tightening her scarf around her neck as they started to cross the river. The boy nodded and then shrugged.

'Use your words, Mitchell.' His mother squeezed his gloveless hand to comfort him. Her daughter chatted away with Megan, who had now moved slightly ahead. Joanna felt a strange pang of rejection, and tried not to think of Martha's smooth grey jackets, free of grass stains. Nor did she dare check her phone.

Mitchell cleared his throat, as if about to make a great speech.

'Yes. Mum always takes us. Normally, we march with one of her friends, but we got here late today.'

'Yeah, mum,' Bert chirped up, whipping around to look at her mum. 'Where's Laura?'

Nesta's face flushed. She wrapped her scarf tighter to her chin. 'At the front. With the others.' Nesta wished she was marching among them, holding the banner and proving to anyone who cared to watch, just how far she'd come on what her mum would have branded her 'silly journey of self-discovery', but the LNER services have a knack of ruining your dreams, and so she was marching with the sort of women she had always felt rejected by.

'I'm sorry you missed your group,' the young woman in the blue coat smiled kindly, her nose bright red in the cold, her frown one of concern. 'I hate marching alone, there isn't anyone to talk to. Ben comes with me,' she patted the shoulder of the man beside her, who was waving his sign with gusto.

'Thing is,' Ben said, 'Megan ends up talking to everyone! I don't think you can say you're alone on a march like this.'

'Hear, hear,' Joanna chimed in. 'A best friend can be made on a march and yet never seen again.'

Nesta thought this was all well and good, and refrained from mentioning an SWP march in Salford where she had been almost trampled underfoot by enthusiasts, when a rumour went up that a sympathetic celebrity was cycling alongside them. But then, that was the day Laura had knelt down and become part of Nesta's life, as quickly, simply and trustingly as her little Bert had taken to the furrowed-browed, blue-coated woman in front.

'I'm Megan,' the blue-coat held out a hand and Nesta, sandwich board against elbow, grasped it.

'Nesta.'

'I'm Bert, and this is Mitchell,' the little girl piped up.

'And this is Ben and Joanna,' Megan introduced her rally family to the upturned chin beside her.

Megan felt a little choked up. She missed her mum. Ben's warmth beside her was a comfort, but Joanna's melancholy presence offered a solace she didn't think she'd feel today, marching as they all were towards the edge of the abyss. And the new woman, Nesta, she seemed sad too, downcast, downtrodden... knackered. Megan's arm already hurt from Bert's attention, and they hadn't even crossed the bridge yet.

All around her, Megan's home town sprawled. A city with a routine that ran on plastic and petrol that could be smelt all around the world. Even with the bridge closed, the sun glinting off cars and trains hurt her eyes, the roar of the planes constantly overhead hummed in her ears.

Standing there over the Thames, Megan felt a wave of inadequacy wash over her. Bert tugged her hand, excitedly pointing at the London Eye.

Joanna shrugged, told Bert to look the other way: 'At the beauty that is St Paul's Cathedral. Not for any religious reason. Just for sheer grandeur.'

Nesta glanced at the quiet, elegant building. Mitchell shrugged. 'I like the Shard.'

'A phallic symbol, if ever I saw one,' Joanna admonished. Megan raised her eyebrows at Mitchell's confusion.

'But it is really shiny,' Bert added, much to Nesta's relief. She laughed quietly into her scarf and raised her chin slightly, weirdly proud of her infants' perceived lack of taste and her son's happy admiration for such a priapic skyline. As she looked back down from the shining spear, her eyes caught sight of a rainbow coloured banner, lower at one corner than the other.

Nesta's heart beat hard beneath her sandwich board. *Laura*.

'Laura!' Nesta shouted above the chanting, cheering, laughing crowd, looking for the flash of red of Laura's dyed ponytail.

'Laura!' Bert squeaked, jumping to try to see through the crowd.

'Lauraaaaaa!' Mitchell whined, his nose still dripping profusely.

'Laura!' Joanna barked, hoping this would cheer up the dopey Nesta.

'Laura!' Ben bellowed, enjoying himself without really being able to explain why.

'Laura!' Megan croaked out, struggling to shout a name so familiar to her. A name she adored and yet rarely used. A name synonymous with 'mum'. 'Laura!' she continued, strengthened by Ben's hand on hers. 'LAURA!' she cried.

Joanna jumped at the force of Megan's shout. Her Ben seemed unperturbed, but had his arm wrapped around her shoulders. The rest of the group fell silent as she shouted the name again, and again. It was as if she were deflating. She hollered repeatedly, until there was a crack in her voice, and then a pitch just that was just short of tears.

Ben supported her as she screamed.

Nesta watched, aghast.

Bert let go of Megan and returned to the relative safety of her mother's sandwich board.

'Laura!' Megan croaked, the volume rapidly decreasing. 'Laura?' It was almost a question. Ben, unable to answer it, hugged her close to him as she finally gave up and fell quiet.

Nesta looked at Joanna, whose mouth twisted in discomfort at the awkward silence that had fallen. The march jostled and moved around their uncomfortable bubble.

The group started to move again.

After a moment or too, Mitchell burst the atmosphere with an elongated: 'Muuuuum?'

'Not now, Mitchell,' Nesta sighed, still looking towards the colourful banner that was moving further away.

'But…' Mitchell paused. 'But m–'

'Nesta?' A vibrantly red head of hair forced its way back towards Nesta and her children. She kissed Nesta fiercely on the mouth and Joanna, finally seeing a smile on Nesta's face, sighed.

'Laura,' Nesta gasped in air. 'This is Megan,' – a tearful nod – 'and Ben,' – a friendly smile – 'and Joanna.'

'Lovely day for it, isn't it?' Laura grinned, hoisting Bert onto her hip and ruffling Mitchell's hair. Mitchell was transfixed, however, with a sign behind them.

'Mu-um,' he whined, glancing at Nesta. 'Muuuum!' Mitchell was growing impatient now, fed up with being ignored: 'MUUUUM!'

'What is it, Mitchell?' Nesta asked, still gazing at Laura, 'You're screaming like it is the end of the world or something!'

Megan started to laugh. Joanna's mouth twitched up. Bert snuggled into Laura's scarf.

The sun shone over London. Joanna thought of Martha, Nesta and Laura hugged. Bert hit Mitchell, who pinched back. Ben worried about Megan. Megan thought about her mum, and raised her placard high.

El Gordo
(There is safety on our island)

Jane jumped as the air conditioning hummed into action. Sitting in front of the machine, she let the air dry the sweat sticking her shirt to her body. Pelayo, her co-worker, grinned at her. His cigarette, stuck to his bottom lip, dripped ash onto his desk.

'*Joder!*' He swore, rubbing the ash from the page. She wheeled herself back to her desk, afraid to stand in case she had sweat patches anywhere else. She raised an eyebrow at her colleague.

'The application form for daughter of the *alcalde*,' he waved the ash-stained document at her. 'I have made a mess of it. He won't be very happy.'

She grinned.

'Do not laugh at me!' he warned, his head tilted. 'What is funny, *la rubia?*'

She thrilled to the nickname, in the same way that she thrilled to all the comfortable, happy signs of belonging in this place. She frowned.

'That word – *alcalde*,' Jane laughed. 'In Spanish lessons at school, we used to use it to say what we would do if we were mayor. To talk about hypothetical situations.'

Pelayo sat back, hands behind his head, two sweat-stained armpits on show. He frowned at her to continue. Jane knew he liked the stories about how she came to speak Spanish.

'For example, *si fuera alcaldesa*, if I were mayor, I would apply to escape to Great Britain even though I have no repatriation rights…'

Pelayo sat forward, a ready grin on his face. 'I would get a non-smoker to complete my immigration forms.'

Jane laughed. 'I wouldn't put my life in the hands of two bored post-graduates.'

'I never graduated,' Pelayo leaned across the desk. 'They hired me due to my charm and wit.'

The air conditioning's hum abruptly stopped.

'*Joder!*' Pelayo stood up, marched towards the machine, removed a flip-flop and began to beat the vented box with all the frustration of the day.

Jane put her hands to her ears and stared at her inbox. Today, her job, funded by the English and supported by the Spanish, had consisted of deleting over twenty emails from desperate ex-pats, begging for passage back to England. Ex-pats who were finding the sun that they had sought just a little too hot and their new home just a little too dangerous. Ex-pats who now looked for solace in the lies fed to them by British politicians.

There is safety in our island nation.

Or *isolanation*, as Jane liked to think of it.

Now that the air-con was whirring again, Pelayo had retired to the courtyard. Jane watched the smoke from his cigarette drift past the window, coiling ever upwards to join the smog that hung over Oviedo. Smog that was made in the congested industrial machine that barely kept the continent alive. Smog that was allowed to thrive in the oppressive heat of the sun and the haze of an evaporating Atlantic that was now as warm as the Mediterranean. Jane could still remember the toe-numbing blue of the ocean in which she'd paddled as a child, on holiday in Europe. A time when the continent had seemed, to her, an extension of England. A given, very rarely considered, part of her future.

If she tried, Jane could just about remember the bracing sea spray, the cold salty tang at the back of her throat, the cry of seagulls that sent her and her sister keening across the sand, their arms aloft.

The heavy, beige mist covered Spain, from A Coruña to Cadiz. It covered the rest of Europe, uniting all nations under its haze. Now both the Union and the continent were again bound together. Under the same dirty sky, England strove to once more befriend Europe, in the descent towards disaster.

Jane took off her glasses and rubbed her eyes. Half blind, she opened her desk drawer slightly. Even with her blurred vision, her blue British passport shone up at her. Its front cover was sleek with under-use, unlike all her other passports. Those beloved maroon books. The last time she saw a passport that colour was at the airport, when she arrived back into Spain. They took it from her.

At eighteen, she had thrilled at applying for her first adult passport. And when it arrived, it was a beautiful thing to hold in her hand, warm with adventure. Its corners had become bent from the constant stuffing into backpacks on her various inter-railing expeditions. Its tattered pages had been littered with stamps. She still remembered having the photo taken, with a boyfriend standing behind the shop assistant and making stupid faces. Her smile was slight, kept down at the corners (just). She had been about to embark on her first, parent-free adventure, with said funny-faced boy. It was a time when Europe had been her own personal playground, nightclub, bar, lifestyle.

Jane growled. She slammed the drawer, jammed her glasses back on, went back to watching Pelayo pick at something in his teeth. Wondered how long she had left to enjoy Pelayo's bad manners.

She looked down at the pile of Application for Repatriation to Great Britain forms, sticking to her elbow with sweat. What would she do, if she had to complete a form like this? What if her passport were a different colour?

Name: Jane Smith. Couldn't get more English than that, could you?

Age: 35. Old enough to know what was happening to the world, to understand what the news was telling them about ice-caps and *El Niño*. Old enough to be partly responsible for what was coming. Too young, she felt, to die.

Nationality: British – but could she also put Spanish? How could she fit how deeply she loved this corner of Europe into a box the size of a tick? And how could she explain that she didn't want to belong to her 'island nation' anymore?

Occupation (in this box, please explain why you think your occupation should allow you re-entry into Great Britain):

Here, Jane became unstuck. She watched Pelayo through the window as he stamped out his cigarette. She should never have left England. Not again. Not having already had, as her parents and sister put it, her European youth, not with the knowledge she had of the division, climate change, political upheaval – but they couldn't stop her, not her family, not the foreign office – not herself. They'd had to let her go.

Jane had to be honest with herself – she knew she hadn't planned on returning.

At the airport, where planes were constantly being grounded, and policemen with huge guns roamed, her mum had pinched her cheek, her dad had told her it would do her good to feel important. Her sister had hugged her, looking away. Helen had never quite understood the desire to constantly be elsewhere. Jane's elder sister was one of those people who had been content, every time, to sit backwards when travelling by train. Jane, however, always wanted to look ahead, to find the next adventure.

By the time her plane touched down between the Picos de Europa, in verdant, windy Asturias, Jane knew she had made the right choice. Shortly after her arrival, the UK government passed what the pundits still call the government's 'tantrum trap'. For Jane, it meant that if she came back to England from Spain, she would never be allowed to return.

Jane put her hand to her face, thought of her mum's touch. Did she feel important? Was this doing her good?

'You think too much, *mija*. Just remember, let the computer choose for you.' Pelayo was leaning against the doorframe, a fleck of tobacco in his moustache.

Pelayo had had this epiphany a few weeks back. His head buried in a stack of applications, he had jumped up, dragged the bin to his desk and swept them all in.

'You need to recycle,' Jane had reprimanded him, making them both howl with the futility of it all.

'Stop reading,' he'd ordered, when they'd finished their giggle. Jane, happily, had taken her glasses off and rubbed her tired eyes while Pelayo explained his plan. Over the next few days, they put the names of all the applicants into a programme that randomly selected data. Now, every morning, in homage to the once adored El Gordo, they played the lottery with individual futures. They printed boarding passes for the lucky winners. They waited for the phone call from the British government that would surely shut them down.

'Have you put your name into it?' Jane had asked him, on the first day that they had played at being bureaucracy gods.

'*Joder, mujer*,' Pelayo had grinned. 'I'll never be British.'

*

They quit work at six. Jane waited outside whilst Pelayo set the alarm. She couldn't wait for a *caña*. The sun worked its way through the heavy cloud to cook the concrete beneath her dirty, sandalled feet. All she could think about was the bead of moisture running down the side of the glass, the bitter lemon José always added for her, *la inglesa*.

'*¿Vamos?*' Pelayo asked, turning the key for the final time. They crossed the square and headed into Al Extranjero.

Pelayo held the door open for Jane. As they entered, Juan and Mari-Sol, the old married couple who owned the flat Jane rented, nodded at them from the corner.

'*Cuatro cañas*,' Pelayo told José. José, Pelayo had always said, was a proper Asturiano. '*Con la sidra que corre en su sangre*,' Pelayo had informed her, with a wink. José, shaking his fist at the television above the bar, did not look as though his veins bled cider.

Jane never could tell if what Pelayo said was idiomatic, or just Pelayo-isms. Either way, Jane loved his stories, his deep Asturian tones. She'd once told him that. She'd been met with laughter.

While Pelayo waited, he leant against the counter, rolling another cigarette. Jane hopped up on a stool, letting her toe scud the ground. She rubbed her eyes, slipped her glasses back on and accepted her cool drink with gratitude. Pelayo stepped outside with Juan and lit up.

She let her eyes drift to the TV in the corner. The British Prime Minister was speaking with a wrinkled, blighted face. In the left corner of the screen, a graphic was plotting the torturous path of the Great Wall of America. Along the bottom, a ticker striped news of nuclear tests and descriptions of the poisonous effects of the Euro smog. Jane took another sip. How well she remembered laughing at the news in the past. Jeering at other governments for electing ridiculous, pampered leaders. How much better she'd felt then about the UK, once the other countries were showing their own true colours.

Jane had come to realise that her true colours were red and yellow.

'You're like Hemingway,' a fellow student (English) had told her once when she'd told him about her love of all things Iberian. 'All talk and no action. Running to the defence of what you imagine to be the suffering Spaniard.' At the time, she'd run to her own defence.

She looked at Pelayo as he stepped back into the bar, lifting his arms to the air conditioning and running a broad hand through his hair. She wasn't rushing to anyone's defence. He wasn't suffering. It felt, often, that it was all quite the opposite. Catching her smile, he made his way back to the bar, slapping Juan on the shoulder as he passed.

'*¡Qué coño!*' Pelayo leant beside her, nodding towards a suited politician, now filling the screen. With panicked hand movements, he seemed to be explaining the predicted effects of *El Niño*, currently reaching its peak in the Pacific. Jane turned so that their elbows touched as they watched the scientific diagram on the screen play out. Pink arrows tangled with blue, a model of the ocean rose, and rose, and rose – and then fell on a cartoon picture of a town. Next appeared a map of Spain, with arrows pointing to Gijón, Asturias' second city.

Pelayo nudged her shoulder with his forehead – just for a second. Jane looked away from the television. She took another long drink and sighed.

'What are you going to do next?' she asked him. She looked at the heavy, sweaty, sweet-scented head beside her. She rubbed her eyes beneath her glasses, took another drink.

'Find some more work. Drink some more beer. Eat some tortilla.' He motioned at José, who bought them over a plate of *pinchos*. 'Meet another *inglesa* on a mission to change the world.'

Jane snorted into her small slice of *tortilla de patatas*.

'Not sure there is much left to change, now,' she nodded up at the screen. She sipped away the worry biting at her throat. The sinking feeling that urged her to think of home, the island. Those men and women in suits, gesticulating wildly from screens, told her that there is always safety to be found on the island.

What about her island, here? Her little bar with Pelayo and José, her desk and the wonky air-conditioning?

'I think I might stay here,' Jane announced to the bar.

Pelayo shrugged, but the smile on his face betrayed his glee at the idea.

'You say that every night, *mija*,' Pelayo informed her, and put his hand out. 'And it's your round.'

A Good War?

The applause in Durham is good. Not as good as last week's at the symposium in London, but much better than last month's reception in Edinburgh. No chance of me travelling further afield. The Committee deemed it unsafe for a scientist to travel abroad these days. Especially a climate scientist. Especially to Europe. My dreams of a month on the continent were quickly quashed.

There is no one standing and cheering, whistling at me with all their might, that just doesn't happen at these sorts of things. It isn't like an end-of-school-year show for parents, or a Nativity play. As I smile and nod at the crowd, I pretend that somewhere in the lecture theatre is my dad, cheering me on as though I am twelve and have clumsily made it through a pitiful rendition of Moon River. The familiar thought makes my laugh genuine, the relief of this circuit of tours almost being over, palpable, the dread of what comes next, minimal.

At this conference, I am allowed to sit down for the audience questions. Which is good, because I am too new in academia to wear those almost-trainers I've seen on colleagues' feet. The type you can only order from websites, the type made from felt. My brogues are as stiff as they are sensible, and these last few months have done nothing to break them in.

The same could be said about me, I suppose.

The host isn't the university Vice Chancellor for a change. Instead, I have hard-headed, myth-busting journalist Jaimini Strickland, PhD, to grill me. And grill me she will. Her name is rarely far from the by-lines of breaking news. I look down at her feet, my throat dry. Her shoes are felt free. I look up and see that her eyes are sharp and clear. She stares unblinkingly into the spotlight, a woman used to many years in front of an audience, albeit invisible under the projector's glare.

'I will open to the audience very soon,' she declares in an enviably arresting voice, 'but first, I must ask you, Doctor Williams, if you could explain the title of your book a little more. Why did you name it *A Good War?*'

'Because my publisher told me to,' I say. The few laughs I receive are quickly drowned out by a serious silence of brain power. These people don't have time for humour. I take a sip of water, decide to tell the truth.

'It is what my grandmother said once. She used to live near a school for boys and one afternoon while she was shopping, her garden was completely ruined by some local teenagers.'

Bulbs ripped out. Grandma crying. The holly under which we'd buried Bruce the dog was slashed to pieces.

25

I blink in the light. The audience says nothing. Their attention does not feel kind. It is Strickland's fault, she's the one who has seen through me, who has asked a 'non-academic' question about my book.

'In the heat of the moment, she'd been furious with the young boys who'd done it. She took me to one side and said: what this country needs is a good war.'

There are a few assenting sounds out in the dark. I open my hands out to the ceiling.

My host looks nonplussed, unimpressed. A raised eyebrow urges me on.

'I think she believed that if the boys had been forced to go to war, the bored teenagers would have had structure, an outlet...' I swallow. *Man alive* – my brain sparks – *I sound pro-war!* '...but I don't think she really meant it.' No response. Keep going, I'm making a mess of this. I soldier on, 'a-and I am sure my grandmother would never have wanted our next battle to be one of climate crisis.' Brought it back to the topic. Nice.

Doctor Strickland smiles at me, now that she has the answer she wants. The audience shifts en masse, obviously unimpressed. I feel, all over again, my inadequacy at all this front-of-house stuff. I had begged the Committee to choose anyone but me, to put me back in the lab, or in front of a screen of graphs.

The lights go up in the auditorium. Now that they can be seen, people remove their fingers from their noses, slip their phones back into their pockets. Strickland motions for the roving mics to head towards the hands that suddenly shoot up. *Here goes.*

But before questions can be asked of me, by anyone, the room goes dark, and I hear heavy boots cross the stage. There is a presence behind me, one in front of me. There are hands all over me. They lift me, all seventy kilos of me, out of my chair. I feel flying and faint. My brogues scuff along the ground as I am dragged off stage.

No one defends me. No one shouts out for help.

*

My glasses are taken, and someone slips a blindfold over my head. I am put in the back of a car. Not thrown, but placed, quite gently really.

'Don't take it off,' the stranger says to me in a low growl, full of intent. 'If you do, I'll hurt you.'

The knot forces my hair clip to dig sharply into my scalp, but aside from that, I am unharmed. Am I relieved to have missed the Q and A session? Or is this alternative worse? There is a disturbing parallel between being asked unknown questions in front of an over-intelligent crowd and being driven blind through a city you don't know. I'm going to miss my train.

Of course this is worse. From what I can tell as we drive, there are two Presences. One sounds young, self-assured, certain. He is the one who threatened me. The other sounds older, slower – concerned. I lift my hand to the fabric around my face.

'Don't you dare touch that blindfold,' the younger voice, no kinder due to its youth, reminds me. I let my hand fall to my side and, trying not to appear anxious, I tap it about the car-seat, to find the seat belt. Safety first. My hand touches something warm and cushioned, fleshy and alive–

'I don't hold hands on the first kidnapping.'

I reel my hand in, my cheeks go red even though I can't see who it is laughing at me.

'S-sorry,' I manage, my voice sounding far away.

The person beside me (a woman, I think) laughs.

'Where am I?'

'Wherever they picked you up.' She sounds bored. 'The car hasn't moved yet.'

'Are we still outside the conference centre?'

'How would I know?' She is angry. 'I can't bloody see either.'

The car lurches into movement. We both stop talking in a vain attempt to use our other senses to work out where we are being taken. I count on my right hand every right turn we take, and do the same with my left. Except, that doesn't work, does it? Because was my first count on the right hand or was it on the left? What would I say to a potential saviour? We took three lefts and four rights, but I can't tell you in which order. I begin to feel something akin to panic. Not quite there yet. Panic's agitated cousin. Rain and wind hit the car sideways. Inside though, it is almost too warm.

*

'You can take the blindfolds off now.'

We do as we're told.

The Presences swim into view. Blurry figures, without my glasses. One leans over, hands them to me. I slide them on. I gasp at my renewed vision. I shake out my damp hair, shiver with the recent wind-chill.

Two men, one young, one older. Both have the same round, brown eyes that narrow when they speak. Kind eyes, worried eyes.

The older man offers me a cup of tea, which I accept. I look about, letting the liquid warm my fingers. We're in a living room. A lived-in living room. There are photo frames containing family pictures that I can't quite pick out at a distance, my eyes still blurry. There are cornices and bookshelves and a shining metal dish of pine-cones in the fireplace. From time to time, a rush of wind storms down the chimney, causing the dish to rattle against the tiles.

'N-nice place,' I say. The older man inhales sharply, stares at me with watering eyes. Behind him, the curtains are drawn, but I can glimpse the grey sky. There is a mirror to the left of the window. Is that pathetic looking woman me? Why does she let her hair hang over her face like that, like some protective brown curtain? Look at them, not at me!

'Is it poisoned?' The woman beside me sniffs her cup. The young boy shakes his head so earnestly, she seems to believe him. She takes a sip and looks over at me. She raises an eyebrow:

'They must want something, so why kill us?' She shrugs, takes a second, huge slurp, 'Aaah, lots of sugar. That's a good cup of tea.'

I take an apprehensive sip. She's not wrong. I try to put my shoulders back, to build a power pose.

The men watch us, as if unsure as to their next step.

'You've not done this before.' The woman beside me has a throaty yet effortless laugh. I can't help but smile. The younger man catches my eye and under the weight of such a glorious chuckle, even his face softens. The older man shrugs, apparently unable to see the levity in the situation.

'Let's hope we don't do it wrong then.'

He pulls a kitchen knife from his back pocket. The me in the mirror escapes back under her hair, flinching inward, shaking hands over her chest. The woman beside me, as brave-looking as I am weak, stops laughing. Puts her tea on the floor beside the sofa. I wince at the noise. My brain is concerned: the floorboards aren't varnished.

'Dad, stop it.' The younger man says and perches on the coffee table, pushing a Capital Cities of the World jigsaw puzzle box to one side. A piece slides off onto the rug. They'll never complete it now. The older man puts the knife away, but now we all know it is there. My heart trips – he is in control of that knowledge.

The younger one rests his head on his hand, as if he were leaning down to explain something difficult to a child. His brows seem weighed down with guilt. 'We don't want to hurt you. We just need some information from each of you.'

I look at the woman next to me, blinking quickly. She looks at me. She tries a small smile of warmth. It makes her eyes crinkle up. Her mouth looks comfortable mid-grin, even here, even now.

'It is really great to meet you, Doctor Williams.'

She knows me? I slosh my tea slightly and it soaks into my trousers, dances up some of my split ends. Have I met her? Did we once wo–

'Don't worry.' That great smile again. 'I don't expect you to know who I am.'

Someone worth kidnapping. Embarrassment wraps its hot arms around me. For a moment, there is no space for panic. I clasp my mug, unsure what to say. Then I remember the knife and let out a noise sort of like a sob. Now, I'm blushing again.

'Colleen Nkosi.' She juts her tea-free hand out into my thoughts. As we shake, we both notice that mine is so much sweatier than hers. '*Ms.* No academic title, I'm afraid. Still, I *am* a novelist.' As she says the word, her chest puffs out and she shakes her head like a bird taking a water bath.

'She writes books about the apocalypse,' the younger man says and looks down at his hands. 'They're pretty good actually.' He swallows, 'I – I'm quite excited to meet you, Ms Nkosi.'

That wonderful laugh again.

'And I you,' her voice is hearty, valiant. 'This will make an excellent story.'

'The apocalypse?' I find my voice, pulling it from deep within a closing throat. She looks at me.

'I came to hear your talk. It's research for my next book–'

'The last in the series,' the younger man jumps in. 'The world as we know it is coming to an end and–'

'And so…' Ms Nkosi gives him a look. He goes quiet and his skin reddens. She turns to me, 'I came to see you because I need to know what the end of the world might look like.'

'And so do we.' The older man's voice reminds us, again, of his knifely presence. He stands at the end of the sofa. 'We're hoping you two ladies can help us.'

*

They make more tea. In a tone of voice that is half pleading, half uncertain, I try to convince them that all the data we have, everything written in my book – all of it is conjecture. In a minute voice that has undone months of conference training, I describe how it is all information based on models of expected human behaviour, on the anecdotal case study, of analysing historic environmental patterns. Possibilities based in evidence, drawing on history but–

'…not promises,' I finish in the whisper of a small child. What has happened to me? I refuse to look back in the mirror, to see me trying to hide within my jacket.

The room is silent. No applause this time.

'And what's this information for?' Colleen Nkosi asks, now a part of the interrogation, her empty teacup clutched tightly in one hand. She knows I have something more to say. How does everyone in this room know more than I do?

'Good question, Ms Nkosi,' the younger man nods at his hero. She manages not to roll her eyes. It is a triumph.

'For?' I feel my cheeks get hot. Too much tea, too much attention. The men. That knife. My brain, bursting to find the right verbal route. The path with the right diversions around and bridges over certain information.

I look down at my brogues. 'W-well, for the Committee for Climate Change.

My sponsors. A-and for anyone who is interested in it, I suppose… I mean, I know that some of the evidence has been passed onto the gov–'

Both men start laughing. It is not kind laughter. There is a sharp edge to it, on which I feel I might soon be impaled. They may have pulled the curtains across the handsome bay window, but through the small gap, I can see that it is starting to get dark. How long have we… I… been here? No one has come to find us. Am I collateral? Is she? My throat gets even tighter. I shut my eyes so that I don't see the sides of the room rush in. I am about to give into panic's sweet relief when I feel her hand on mine. I open my eyes to find her leaning toward me. I can see a small bead of sweat drop down her neck into her shirt collar. She's scared too?

'It is okay, Doctor Williams, just tell them what you know.' She squeezes my hand and lets it drop. Independently of my brain, my hand moves to follow hers. There is a silence, in which all four of us witness this and pretend we haven't.

She coughs, smooths down her skirt.

The room rumbles as the central heating comes on.

'We've got all the time in the world, doc,' says the older man. He crosses the room, walks out the door. I hear the sound of keys turning, of the front-door chain being slid into place. 'Although the planet might disagree.'

'No rush, is there Dad?' calls the younger, taking his phone out of his pocket and snapping a picture of us.

We both open our mouths to complain, but the photographer raises his hand–

'Tell us the truth.'

'What are you going to do with that picture?' I ask.

'Send it to some people we know.'

'People?'

'Mean people. Thugs.' The younger one says it quietly. He looks straight at me. 'Some boys who could do with a really good war.'

I see my grandma's ruined garden. I see my dad's concerned face. I see my nephew laughing at a tulip. I see blood.

'Wesuppliedthedatatoagovernmentschemeaimedatbuildingdefences.' Unstoppable, unslowable, the truth tumbles out of my mouth. I take in huge gulps of air.

'Sorry… what was that?' The older man joins his son at the coffee table. It creaks under their combined weight. The younger man taps on his phone for a moment and then slides it across the floor towards the sofa. Ms Nkosi looks at me. I look at her.

He is recording.

'We supplied the data to a government scheme – an agency really – that is working to build defences.'

'Defences?' questions the older man.

'A-against what's coming…' I stammer.

'And what is coming?' Ms Nkosi asks.

'The apocalypse.' Says the younger man.

*

They let us wee in a downstairs toilet which smells of lavender and is painted apple green. They give me a break while they question Ms Nkosi on her research, her connections with scientists, what she knows about the government's plans for us all. I listen to them grilling her, a puddle of sweat. Predictably, her knowledge is patchy. They know that I can fill in the gaps. Before they come to me, they heat up some frozen pizza. Pepperoni. I find myself wanting to tell them that I am a vegetarian, that if we're trying to save the world all this meat and cheese isn't going to help matters. I have to bite my tongue against the desire to disturb the precarious peace that descends.

'So, what are your novels called?' I ask Ms Nkosi, trying to catch my breath.

'The *Goodbye to Gaia* saga,' the younger man jumps in, and Ms Nkosi nods.

'A great title,' I say, and she narrows her eyes slightly, nods again.

Silence. Unbearable silence, in which there are no sounds of hostage negotiators or neighbours we could scream for.

'That is a nice photo,' I try again. My voice is still small, my closed throat making it impossible for me to eat. The older man follows my wavering gaze and points to the photo I am looking at, the one I can't really see.

'That's my wife, Clém's – his mum.' he nods at the younger man, who is busy dipping his crusts in mayonnaise. He smiles goofily up at us. The older one continues, 'She used to work in IT communications, for the government.'

My eyes meet Ms Nkosi's. The way he said 'used to'.

'Wh-what does she do now?' I swallow, ripping at the crust of my pizza with shaking hands.

'She was disappeared.' The younger one, his mouth still slightly full, looks over at the photo. 'She was too good at her job or… she knew too much.'

'Too much about wh–'

The older man bends to slam his hand on the coffee table and a piece of pizza flies from Ms Nkosi's open mouth. I push my shoulders into the back of the sofa as he leans in towards me over the half-empty plates. 'You don't ask the questions. You don't get to pity me. You and your kind are the reason she is mis – she is gone.'

He's pointing at me with a steady, ruthless finger. He's got a wedding ring on. *Me and my kind.*

Ms Nkosi bends down from her perch on the sofa to pick up the stray pizza.

'I am so sorry,' she starts, her menace-free voice a huge contrast to his loud

31

overtones. 'It must be awful, not knowing.'

All three of us nod, even though she is not talking to me. Even so, it is awful, not knowing.

'But forgive me.' Ms Nkosi sounds so certain that they will. 'Surely Doctor Williams is an expert, like your wife was – is?'

I am an expert? Nausea arrives, the nausea caused by me realising how far out of my depth I am. I am an expert?

'My wife believed in something other than data,' the older man shakes his head, leaning back and putting his hand into his back pocket. Ms Nkosi and I both sit up straighter, covering our torsos as best we can with our arms.

'Protecting the world. Celebrating it. Prevention, rather than cure.' The younger man speaks up now, his eyes damp. 'She loved your books, Ms Nkosi.'

They smile at each other. I am finding it harder to control my breathing.

*

The younger man takes Ms Nkosi to another room. He doesn't touch her, but something in his sudden change of stance makes it clear she must go with him. He is taller than her and her power diminishes as she is forced to follow him out. She turns to look at me, tries another small smile.

The older man'll get it all out of me. I can't help it. What could happen to my family, my nephew? He's barely able to talk – what does he care about my research? And, what about me? What about her? I have to make a decision between definitely losing my life now, or maybe losing my life later.

The older man cracks his knuckles, checks his phone, puts his nose inches from mine and then, passing the knife between his hands, forces me to divulge it all.

He starts by asking me about the time scale. Time limit, rather.

'We are predicting huge changes, within two years.' I tell him, looking at my pale hands in my grey lap. The lifelines are vivid pink, my quickened pulse making them throb. He swears, readjusts his position.

'What do you mean by huge changes?'

'El Niño is going to wreak some havoc.' I wedge a thumbnail between my teeth, trying to put a stopper on the facts desperate to escape my mouth.

He waves the knife under my nose, leans across to me. 'Try harder, Doc,' he hisses in my ear. My hairs rise at his pizza breath.

'The sea level is going to rise and rise.' I push myself back into the sofa. 'There is this ice cap in Greenland, and it is melting, it will melt. A-and that will lead to flooding of towns and cities along the coast of England. It will be slow at first but–'

'How high?' he asks, his voice a growl.

'W-well, in the first stage, we predict a rise of u-up to... of around seven metres and then–'

'How high?' He asks again, the knife clenched in his hand.

I stare the floor. At my shoes. At his trainers. My voice is tiny: 'Thirty metres within the next decade.'

He grunts in disbelief.

'Ms Nkosi predicted that, you know.'

I shrug at him, 'I've not read her books.'

'I can tell.' He narrows his eyes at me.

I ask him about Ms Nkosi's books. He tells me that his wife's favourite in the saga was all about the deadly power of the ocean. He smiles when he thinks of her and his hand loosens around the knife. I let myself breathe.

'Does Ms Nkosi mention the rogue waves?' I ask, in what I realise too late is a pique of jealousy. What on earth am I jealous of? My cheeks flush. He stares at me.

'Rogue waves?'

'O-or freak waves.' Now that I have started telling the truth, I can't seem to stop myself. 'And does she also write about the certain famine? And the body count?'

He barks a laugh. 'People only worry about the body count if there is a specific body that is part of it. The only body that counts is my wife's.'

I force myself to look at him. 'You don't know she's dead.' My back is slick with sweat.

'I don't know she's not.' He sighs, rubs his forehead with his free hand. The knife remains pointed at me, pressed between his palm and the coffee table.

'Not knowing is hard,' I try to sound kind, but the words come out bitter.

'Which is why we're here today.' His voice is quiet. My head hums as I nod, not knowing how to continue, but wanting to tell him everything. To tell someone everything. Fortunately, he is not finished either. 'So what is the government cooking up then, to sort all this out?'

'The defence plan is—'

'Wait a second, they're calling it a 'defence' plan?'

I lift my palms up to the ceiling, frustrated at the interruption.

'Typical,' he scoffs. He makes circular motion with his knife hand, telling me to continue.

'The defence plan is, as far as I can tell, to head to higher ground.' *Turn, and if you can, run.* He frowns at me. I persevere, shutting my eyes as I talk, disbelieving the sound of my own voice as I explain about the number of Towers – where they will be built (near-ish coastal areas, so as to take advantage of wind, solar and hydropower), where survivors will live, how they will live. The need for the 'right sort' of architect. And now I can't stop myself. It is vomit, it spews out of me, hot and chunky with facts. I drone on and on about the structure and membership of the new government. The ongoing development of a dual system, with the big decisions being made by those in the Tower and enforced by a skeleton government down below.

'They call it the Power from the Tower / Hand on the Land concept.' I finally finish, making air quotes with my fingers so as to distance myself from his wrath.

'Who gets to go up?'

I put my hand to my throat, feel my heart beat there.

'There will be a lottery.'

'People won't like that.'

People won't have a choice.

'There are lots of spaces. There are lots of Towers.'

'Not enough space for everyone though.'

'No.'

'And those that are left behind?'

I can't look him in the eye. I try to gather the same momentum as last time. I attempt to describe the recruitment drive numbers for the army. The advertisements being recorded, the daytime television celebrities involved. The reels of them calling for the hard and strong bodies that will be needed for the fight against the inevitable uprising of those not in the lottery. Muscle to help set up generators for those left, to continue to enforce 'good environmental practices' when the Towers close their doors.

'What is life outside the Towers going to be like?' His hand on the knife is tight, clenched.

'I don't know,' I say, after a moment.

*

'What did the Government give you in return for all this information?' Ms Nkosi is back in the room with us. 'Or did they threaten you like these two?' She sits as far away from all of us as possible, but the sofa is well used, and we can't help slipping towards the centre. Her eyes are red-rimmed, but her chin is stubbornly high. The younger man looks sheepish and his cheeks burn.

All three of them look at me, even though they already know the answer to her question. We are all in control of the facts now.

'Two rooms, in one of the Towers.' I look down at my hands. 'For my family and for me.'

Ms Nkosi shakes her head, outraged. 'So much for a fair lottery!'

I say nothing. I look to the black window, to the door. The metal dish rattles in the hearth. I put my head in my hands.

'We're not going to take that away from you.' The younger boy is back at the coffee table, his head close to mine. His breath is a hum of garlic and oil. I raise my head, look at them all in turn. Think of the knife. Say nothing. Don't make it worse.

'You work for us now.' The older man crosses his arms across his chest, watches Ms Nkosi and I react.

'Y-you're letting us go?' The woman in the mirror who I think is me manages to look up. Both men nod, so obviously related, so obviously a team.

'From this house, at least,' the older man says.

'Thank you,' I say, and I mean it.

'But I write fiction,' Ms Nkosi says, quietly, 'and you have access to all my research now, what more could you–'

'That final book,' the younger one says. 'It needs to be stirring as fuck. It needs to light fires in their hearts.'

'Whose hearts?' we both ask. She looks at me. I look at her.

'Those boys–' the older man nods to his son, 'and girls, excuse me ladies.' We stare at him. 'Those boys and girls who are going to fight against the government, who are going to fight to survive.' He points at me. 'You're going to know what Towers we need to burn down, which ministers we need… to talk to… Everything you know, we'll know too.'

'I'm not as important as you think.' I look down at my brogues, the symbol of my novice steps into the world of the expert.

'You will be,' the younger one says.

'Make sure you are,' the older one agrees.

I can't meet their eyes. I nod at my hands. Ms Nkosi's laughter stomps around the room. 'How's that for pressure?' she grins at me. 'My editor always told me the last book would be the hardest.'

Extraordinary General Meeting

The prefab hut is bursting. Some late-comers have to stand outside and listen in through the windows. The bright young things – Troy and Liesel – from plot number 26 are there, well-groomed heads full of all this no-dig, what's-the-harm-in-long-grass business. Their wrinkle-free foreheads are close together in what looks to be a polite debate, but from what I overheard as I walked in behind them, is actually a quiet, yet truly vicious, domestic argument.

'Evening Nesta,' Colin says as he settles against the window frame beside me. He has had the furthest to walk, all the way from plot 87. Still, he's given up his early-bird chair for unassuming, boring Graham, who has recently been let go from the architecture firm where he worked, according to the allotment grapevine. He seems to have found the steps a bit of a struggle and has turned quite red. Typical Colin, the white-haired knight of Grange Allotment and Garden Association (GAGA).

Louise, *Queen* Louise, who reigns over all of GAGA, is setting up at the front, one hand on her laptop, the other clutching a granola bar made by Judith from number 42. If anyone had been counting, they would know that this is her third delicacy of the evening. Were someone to ask if Louise called this EGM merely for the cake, it would be understandable. We are all thinking it. I plan to take some home for the kids.

A groaning trestle table stands in the corner nearest the door, heaped with delights baked by our thoughtful neighbours. There is a jam jar to put coins in. We've all got full plates. Sam, the famous chef – and one half of the pair who own the corner plot with the green-painted greenhouse – (wo)mans the stall. She frowns down at Melanie and Dave's (from number 12) 'beetroot baps'. They are, as yet, untouched. Something about the deep pink ooze soaking into the recyclable paper platter just doesn't inspire on this tepid, May evening. The bakers of these baps sit a row in front of the huffing and puffing Graham, legs stretched out and crossed at their bare ankles. Sun (or mud)-browned skin on show in the gap where their matching culottes and sludge-coloured Crocs don't quite meet. Dave's reddened fingers suggesting that the weight of this particular culinary failure rests on his shoulders.

'I think everyone is here now, Lou!' calls Elvis, who is known for his globe artichokes and awful manners. He's vaping just outside the door and bubble-gum smoke drifts across the crowd in great pinkish clouds, causing poor Judith (she of the scrumptious and yet healthy granola bars) to cough. Others cough too, in assent to Elvis's comment, or nodding politely their desire to speed this process along.

Louise stands, dressed in her favourite purple fleece, the one with the legend *Head Gardener* picked out in green thread on the back.

'It is so nice to see you all.' Hers is a large voice for such a small woman. It comes from deep within her barrel-like middle. 'Especially at such concerning times.'

'What is going to happen, Lou?'

'Have you heard anything else?'

'Can you tell us what the bloody bastards have decided?'

'Do they think they can just stamp all over us?'

'We have rights, did you tell them we have rights, Lou? Lou?'

It is like a press junket, questions flying thick and fast, she is unblinking in the sudden pop of light of the single strip, that Elvis has decided needed to be switched on. She waits for people to quiet down, looking to Colin, who does well to shush and make silencing grunts.

The murmuring stops. There is a cracking sound as someone takes a bite of one of Michelle's (plot number 2) peanut butter cookies and perhaps loses a tooth. Troy and Liesel are looking at something on her phone, the glow lighting identical scowls across their well moisturised faces.

'I hope you have all had time to read the email that I forwarded yesterday,' Louise continues. 'It is this email that prompted me to call this meeting.' Louise clasps her hands together, to show us all that shit is about to get real. She sighs, heavily. 'But this morning, I received a follow-up email from the Department for Communities and Local Government – the CLG. As I understand it, it was–' and here, Louise revels in a dramatic pause, 'a notification of potential closure.'

The room erupts. Louise allows it, taking a sip from her water bottle. Her hand is shaking, but her cheeks have that glow that betrays excitement. Aside from growing asparagus in huge, out-of-regulation wire structures – drama is what gives her life.

'When?' Colin, fearing the loss of his corner of paradise, forgets himself. These past few years, he has already lost too much.

'Why?' Liesel cries, making Judith, whose eyes are still watering from Elvis's vape attack, raise her shoulders in surprise and clutch at her chest. Troy shakes his head in obvious embarrassment at his partner's outspokenness. Liesel crosses her arms over her mustard corduroy man's shirt and says it again, louder: 'Why?'

Perhaps it is the raising of her not-insignificant chin, or the power in her voice that has us all cringing, but Liesel becomes our new leader. *Why?* we chant at Louise, *why, why, why?*

When everyone has had the chance to fill the close air with their own irate breath, the noise levels drop again. Louise nods at Liesel, seeing in her a future opponent and respecting her for it (and for being able to carry off menswear so elegantly).

Louise coughs, gives Elvis a withering look (the bubble-gum smoke has reached her corner) and then proceeds:

'The Government wishes to renovate our site. Apparently, it is the exact width and length for them to build nearby, to construct–'

Some tutting, some shushing, some groaning. Elvis bringing a tear to Judith's eye with his choice of swear words.

'–the northernmost Leg,' brave Louise swallows, 'of this region's Tower.'

Silence. The silence of a broken people. Of a lost people. Of a people torn between what is the right thing to do and their deepest, darkest, vegetable-producing desires. Graham lets out a gasp (or perhaps he has finally caught his breath). Judith sighs loudly. Colin, who has always fancied Judith, let's be honest, takes this as his cue.

'How did you respond, Lou?' he asks, moving to the front. It is a natural move and one that Queen Louise of GAGA allows because Colin had run the joint for a decade before she got involved.

'I haven't yet,' Louise looks out at all of us, her eyes brimming and yet, frequently glancing towards the cake table. Colin nods.

'Good, let's ignore the bastards.' Elvis, of course. His large form blocks most of the light and air coming from the door. Perhaps Judith is wondering if it is her destiny to die by the inadequacies of this walking lime-green windbreaker.

'I can't believe I'm going to say this,' Melanie draws herself up to full Pilates-practised height, 'but I agree with Elvis–'

'Here now, why wouldn't you agree with me?' Elvis puffs, Judith coughs, Melanie shifts. 'I always speak sense! Here, you weren't disagreeing with me when I fixed yer bleeding greenhouse, were ya?'

'He's got a point, Mel,' says Dave, the beetroot killer. Mel purses her lips, the bottom one wobbles slightly. Dave goes to put his arm about her shoulders, but she slaps him away.

'Yes, we should protest,' says Judith calmly. Everyone pays attention, because she used to be a head teacher at the primary school my Bert and Mitchell attend. 'But the Towers are going to save people's lives, aren't they?'

'We'll need somewhere to live, if we believe what they're saying on the news–'

'What's the point of living without our plots–'

'I spent too much time manuring to give it all up now–'

Louise waves at the crowd, but no one pays her any attention. She looks up at Colin, beseechingly. He shrugs, nods. She scurries off to the cake table while he claps his hands together.

'It appears that we all – understandably – feel very strongly about this,' Colin nods, his arms tight around his short wax jacket. There are cries from the group, Elvis shouts a string of profanities. 'We should all have the right to speak.' Colin glances behind him, looking for something. He spots what he needs and bending, picks up a tomato cane. He holds out the bamboo stick to the crowd. It sits light in his lithe fingers.

'If you have the stick, you have your say.'

'Here, what is this? The Lord of the fecking Flies?' shouts a characteristically obnoxious, but surprisingly well read, Elvis.

Colin lets himself laugh. The rest of the group follow suit. Louise sidles back up to Colin's elbow, half a brownie in her mouth. Elvis, looking chuffed with himself, takes another long drag.

Graham stands shakily, his cheeks now a pale red, an almost pink. The colour of a rhododendron in first flush. He reaches his hand out and Colin, with gravitas and solemnity appropriate to the situation, hands the cane over.

'Hello everybody, I'm Graham and I am an alcoholic.'

'Er…different sort of meeting, Graham,' Colin says in his kind way. Troy snorts and Liesel nudges him gently, furiously avoiding making eye contact, her lips doing their level best to stay down at the corners.

'Well, Colin,' Graham looks down at the stick, 'that sort of proves my point, d'you know?'

'A-and what is your point, dear?' Louise asks, her voice thick with the sugar coating the back of her throat.

'Th-that the allotment saved me.'

Silence. Michelle from number 2 is tearing up. Even I feel a lump in my throat.

'After losing my job at the firm and all. It gave me something to worry about, you know?'

Everyone nods. I nod. Elvis says, 'Damn right, son.'

'Something to look after.'

Sam, hidden behind the bun mountain, sighs slightly. I want to ask her where her Colleen is, but her body language suggests now isn't a good time. It's a shame, I could have done with a good chat with the two of them. They're always so optimistic and I need a bit of that, at the moment.

Graham shrugs, hands the stick back to Colin, whose bushy white eyebrows have met above his nose. 'So – you don't want the CLG to go ahead with their plans?'

Graham nods, shrugs again. He sits back down. Mel and Dave clap. Liesel puts her hand up for the stick. Colin passes it back to her by way of Judith. Their hands linger on the wood for a moment. Judith hands it back to me to pass on with a characteristically polite 'Thanks, Nesta!'

'I have just re-read the second email Lou sent and the CLG suggest that our plot is not the only potential area for excavation.'

At the word excavation, Michelle from number 2 starts to blub.

Louise nods, 'You're right, Liesel, they're looking at some areas near the river too, but apparently, ours is nigh per–'

'Here, Louise, you've not got the stick!' Elvis, ever the stickler for the rules, points to the boss in outrage.

'That's okay,' says Colin, fairest-of-them-all, and nods at Louise to continue.

'They say that our allotment, due to the shape and size, is perfect.'

'We know it's perfect!' Elvis hollers. 'That's why we lov–'

'Stick!' Liesel waves the cane at him and turns back to her audience, ignoring Elvis's narrowed eyes, 'I think we should protest. Protest to preserve.'

Protest to Preserve is whispered around the group like a rallying cry at a protest. Do I have it in me to make another placard, I wonder. I could ask Bert to make it as part of an 'art project'…

Dave puts his hand out and Liesel passes the cane.

'Hello everyone,' he says, standing up and nodding bearded chin at every one in turn. 'This may be an unpopular opinion, but it needs to be heard. We need the Towers to be built, don't we? Should we stand in the way of progress?'

It is as if Dave has denied the importance of compost heaps or has suggested that manure has no benefits. The hut erupts in consternation. Even soft-natured Sam with the green paint still on her arms looks irate. She is typing furiously on her phone, frequently glancing back up at the group. She's right to be annoyed – Colleen would have torn Dave apart. As it is, Dave, looks pretty scared. He peers down at Mel who, in turn, looks down at her Crocs. Dave plays with the stick in his hand, but doesn't let it go. He waits for the hordes to quieten:

'They're there to protect us, aren't they? They're being built for us, to house us, to house our families, to keep us safe from whatever might happen next. Look, if you read some of the papers, the future isn't bright–'

'Floods,' Elvis nods in sombre agreement, wresting the stick from Dave's mauve clutches.

'Shortages,' Mel pipes up, looking back up at Dave with renewed admiration. I hear Troy whisper something to Liesel about the couple not having a shortage of beets. I turn my laugh into a cough. Troy grins at me.

'Freak waves,' Graham talks into his hands, which cover his face. The whole group looks around at each other. Behind their eyes, each has a vision of their horticultural masterpiece being crushed under a great weight of water. The crack of panes of glass folding in, the creak of ancient branches bending, the splintering of bamboo canes–

'Elvis, can we not break the stick please, mate?' Colin, ever the diplomat, removes the stick from Elvis's hand. He looks around and his eyes glisten when they alight on heavily bejewelled Judith's left hand, high in the air. Perhaps not appropriate attire for gardening, that hefty wedding diamond, Judith. Best stop smiling so warmly at poor Colin.

In a voice pitched at the perfect volume, she says: 'I think we should vote.'

'Not another referendum–'

'My poor heart can't take it–'

'The price of bedding plants since Brexit has soar–'

Judith – a consummate professional – raises the stick. The group (class?) fall silent. 'A three-way vote.'

'Classic. Who does she think she is? Leader of the opposition?' scoffs Elvis. Liesel and Troy laugh. Even cake-table Sam has to smile.

Louise, who had been hovering behind Colin like a sugared-up infant, steps forward.

'Three way?' She holds up three crumbed fingers and goes to list the options. 'One – yes to the Leg.'

Judith nods, 'With reasonable time to sort through our affairs, of course.' Mel sighs beside her, in awe of Judith's control. Perhaps she is wondering if she can hire her as a live-in governess for her unruly daughters.

Louise nods, holds up finger number two. 'Two – no to the Leg. We Protest to Preserve, as Liesel so cleverly put it.'

Liesel gasps, puts her hand to her chest. 'She knows my name!' she whispers happily to Troy. Louise holds her third finger up: 'Three?'

Judith takes a deep breath. 'Yes.' The group collectively exhales, disappointed. 'But on a few conditions.' Liesel and Troy, who had been flicking through their phones again, look up. Graham, Colin, Mel and Dave all stare at Judith. Michelle blows her nose loudly into a well used tissue. 'They promise us an allotment up in the Tower. A roof garden. A greenhouse. Somewhere to work, somewhere to create...' Judith takes another deep breath and looks over at Graham, who gives her small smile. 'Somewhere to have hope.'

Louise, totally overcome, begins to clap. The rest of us in the hut follow suit and there's Troy and Liesel grinning, Elvis whooping, Graham nodding gratefully at Judith, his new-found mother figure who is going to regret ever having made his quite needy acquaintance. Even I offer a few polite words of assent. Judith nods and smiles through her grimace as Elvis cheers and shakes her roughly on the shoulder.

Colin takes the stick back, leaning it against the wall. Louise places a hand on his arm in thanks, leaving small grease stains on his neat jacket. Heroically resisting the urge to wipe them off, he resumes his position at the windowsill.

'Okay GAGA gang,' Louise, refreshed and riding a sugar high, picks up her notebook. 'We'll do it the old-fashioned way. One slip of paper, one vote per person.' She tears a few pages out of her notebook. Judith stands, smoothes down her linens and goes over to help Louise. The paper is soon distributed. The more organised amongst us pass around pens and pencils. We scribble down a 1, a 2, or a 3. We look at each other, quietly pondering whose vote will decide our fate. Troy and Liesel whisper to each other. Mel strains to see what Dave has written.

I write down a 3.

Mitchell would love to live in such a tall building and Bert would adore a roof garden.

And well… we'd be safe, wouldn't we?

Louise, with the help of Judith, collects the votes back in using a tin with *gardeners don't grow old, they just go to seed* emblazoned on the side. She looks over the heads of the crowd and nods at Sam.

'Let's all have some more cake,' Sam stands up, her voice carrying far enough for such an unassuming looking person, 'while Louise gets to counting.' The crowd murmurs its assent, turns towards the trestle table. Dave starts telling Graham all about the wonders of beetroot. Mel gives Michelle a hug, offers her another tissue. Liesel and Troy step outside, standing far enough away from the prefab so as to finish their argument from earlier.

I nip outside for a cigarette.

I watch Elvis walk a little way up the path to the front gate. He takes another vape and surveys the allotments spreading out in front of him. Apple blossom, the last tulip heads, cow parsley – at least, that's what he thinks it is, he suffers quite badly from blepharitis – as far as his eyes can see. He looks at the cake-carrying crowd of his fellow allotmenteers. In the last of the evening sun, his sizeable form casts a long, towering shadow over the lot of us.

Bad Timing

Lloyd hated his name. He told Rhona this on their first date, and then proceeded to list some of the other things he disliked about himself (his lack of any sort of chin, for example). As was the plan, Rhona found this ingratiating behaviour endearing. She had plenty of things she didn't like about herself too (among them, her complete inability to draw a straight line, even with a ruler, and her poor punctuality). Their conversation was comfortable and edifying, and lasted all the way to last orders. They discussed family (his from Newcastle, Geordie born and bred, hers from Islay in the Inner Hebrides), ambitions (both wanted to run their own architects' firm) and even first kisses (his in the playground, in the rain, aged thirteen; hers on a swing in a park in Spain, aged twelve).

They kissed a quick goodbye at the entrance to Monument Metro – the steps to the underground falling away at Rhona's feet. Lloyd decided to walk home along the river – it was a clear night and the lamps on the bridges hummed warmly, the windows of the Byker Wall twinkled ahead of him, his very own northern stars. He thought only about her – her dark hair and the song of her voice. He thought about their next date.

Rhona believed she couldn't get much luckier, but somehow, by West Jesmond, she'd managed to bag her favourite seat on the Metro. The view of the tracks plunging ahead of her made her feel breathless. She kept catching sight of herself in the darkened carriage window and being surprised at her own glee.

That night, both Rhona and Lloyd enjoyed the empty space beside them in bed. Both were sure their time spent alone on this planet was running out.

*

The news about her grandfather's death upset Rhona, but for unexpected reasons. At twenty-three, and with no experience of what was to come, she didn't often dwell on the idea of death. Of course, her throat tightened at the thought of never again seeing his crystal-clear eyes, glaring out as they did from beneath wiry brows, but that wasn't really why she was upset.

What made her really sad was that Fergus, her stoical older brother, was devastated. He and their grandfather – the man who brought them up – had always been close. These past few years, Rhona had been many miles south and east. As the UK became increasingly divided, Rhona worried that her grandfather had seen her life in England as a rejection of his beliefs.

In search of comfort, she made the decision to call Lloyd, and in doing so, sealed their fate. He, still a relative newcomer in her life, was glad she had given him an excuse (albeit a rather sad one) to come over. He leapt at the opportunity to 'be there for her'. He was at her flat within a half hour, which meant he must have taken a taxi all the way to the coast. At least twenty-five pounds, just for her! When the bell rang, she waved him in, her phone clamped to her ear.

'It's my brother,' she explained, ushering Lloyd into the small galley kitchen that she shared with two other students (both postgrads who were out for the evening). She widened her eyes in exaggerated delight at the bottle of wine Lloyd waved in front of her face. Then she mouthed: 'He's talking about the will.'

*

'A distillery? Are you serious?'

'It is the island's economy.'

'But your grandpa owned one? Not just worked in one?'

'A long time ago,' she laughed. 'It was shut down before I was born.'

'Why?'

'Because he enjoyed it too much.'

'It?'

'Whisky.'

'Making it?'

'Drinking it.'

Legs plaited together, opposite each other on her bed, she regaled him with family lore. She described the old stone buildings of the distillery, the musty-sweet scent of drying grain; explained how, on her island, the sea was a constant companion, lapping proprietorially at your wellies, letting you know who was boss.

He sipped some wine. 'I can't imagine you in wellies.'

She rolled her eyes. 'Seeing people in their natural habitat is a privilege.'

'I'd like to see you on your island,' he put a hand on her knee. She took another drink, letting the dormant ache of homesickness awake in her chest.

'So now it belongs to Fergus,' Rhona explained, slightly breathless, motioning at her phone on the bedside table.

'Lucky Fergus,' Lloyd said, in a battle against awkward silence.

'He wants me to help.'

Lloyd raised an eyebrow. He found himself unable to speak. Her last comment, dropped ever-so-delicately into the conversation, happened to be the thing he most afraid of, not that he had known that until now.

At twenty-five and on the cusp of a stellar career in 'building for community' and 'social architecture', he hadn't expected Rhona to step into his life.

But she had.

And now he was petrified that she was about to step back out.

'Come with me,' she asked him, her eyes narrowed, her face set. 'Come and see the real north.'

44

They ventured to the island on a jet of city steam. Lloyd learnt that she had a heavy right foot and that the rental car felt too flimsy for the winding road through the craggy Trossachs.

He learnt that she had an absolute gift of a face, which had the power to fold itself up against the wind. Not to mention a whole cask-load of self-sufficiency.

He discovered, too, that she was even more beautiful in her natural habitat. On her island. In a wild, blustery way.

Rhona learnt that Lloyd was shy of Fergus, who was big and brawny and bellowed every word. Enveloped in his bear hug, she could just see the nervous twist of Lloyd's face over her brother's shoulder.

Rhona also learnt that Lloyd was very good at feigning interest. And that he didn't like the total dark the island had to offer.

As soon as they arrived, Fergus showed them the bog (some of the last remaining peat on the island) and the derelict stone buildings that they now owned. The two young architects pitched in, each with a notion of helping to design the distillery, of getting in on the ground floor.

The first evening of reunion was a late one. Many decisions were made.

Tradition was key.

Do what the ancestors did.

Nostalgia tastes almost as good as single malt.

*

The three of them did countless cask tastings. Distillery buildings were ranked, the advantages of phenol parts per million were roundly discussed. They all wrung their hands repeatedly at the thought of what happened to all the carbon dioxide. Rhona's hopes were writ large across Lloyd's face, frantic with the beauty of the wooden warehouse, his eyes full of alcoholic frenzy as he leant into a washtun and took a huge sniff, the old larch wood straining at its metal rings – he was so happy to be here, on her island.

*

With their soft designing hands, Lloyd and Rhona helped her brother. They spent a tormented week slicing peat from its home. Their peat-cutters had horn-like handles and square metal blades. They were the height of tradition.

One particularly gloomy afternoon, when they took a tea break and the men were talking, Rhona slipped a small corner of the vast field into her pocket. For comfort, later.

As night fell on the last day of the couple's visit (for they were now decidedly a couple) Lloyd and Fergus found Rhona kneeling on the fresh scars of their handiwork, her hands resting palm-up on her knees.

A statue to homesickness.

If they saw her tears, they didn't mention it.

After that week, she stole peat every time she returned home to visit the distillery (and to keep tabs on Fergus). She burnt it over a candle, to help herself feel closer to all the magic of the island.

*

A year later, Rhona proposed to Lloyd in the centre of the Millennium Bridge, one of his favourite places.

It was a bright summer's day and the city was busy, despite the social distancing restrictions still in place after a recent virus flare-up. The sky was the sort of blue that promised a clear night. But, typical Rhona, she got her timing wrong. The bridge, a great white arc of spokes like half a bicycle wheel, rotated 180 degrees every day at a certain time, so as to let boats through. Locals said it looked like the bridge was blinking, its white spokes reminiscent of long eyelashes. When the alarms sounded, bleating warnings to pedestrians and cyclists using the bridge, Rhona continued to shout her proposal. She was determined to receive her answer before coming down off the bridge.

As they were escorted away by men in hi-viz, Lloyd twisted to face her. 'Yes!'

That night, they toasted each other in a pub on the quayside, warming themselves through with a wee dram of single malt.

*

After their wedding – a small secular ceremony which enticed Fergus south of the border – they moved into a bigger flat and quite soon after that, into a house with too many bedrooms. They got a cat – a British short hair called Blueprints. They made money. Quite a lot of money.

The demand for vertical, communal housing soared. The not-so-young architects (now entrepreneurs) took the trip north to Rhona's island less frequently.

They said: we have no time and anyway, the precious cargo is resting. Resting in casks ordered from the USA or mainland Europe and shipped around the globe at £1000 a pop. Made from oak, charred on the inside, infused with the bourbon, or the sherry, they had once borne.

Thankfully – and with additional support from Fergus – their fledgling architect firm was able to support their whisky habit.

*

Their life took on a pattern – together they lived as they thought they wanted to – busy working weeks with business lunches and after-hours meetings followed by busy social weekends meeting friends or potential clients or both. Occasionally, inconveniences flared up, a conference only one of them could attend, a staff member who needed to be sacked for drinking on the job; there were weddings, and their friends started having babies and demanding visits.

Rhona and Lloyd promised each other one weekend a month together, away from it all.

One such Saturday morning, while Lloyd dozed on his front in bed beside her, Rhona read an article in a reputable publication about the negative impact the Scotch industry was having on Douglas fir colonies in Oregon. She didn't tell him, and used the paper for the cat's litter tray.

That same weekend, while she was on the phone to Fergus, Lloyd read an article from a trusted source online about how leftover whisky spirit was dumped into the sea beside the distilleries.

He declined to share the article with her.

*

On the week of her thirtieth birthday, Fergus called his sister. Rhona was still at work in the studio they had set up in the back bedroom. Her lamp was flickering, the generator about to give out, when her phone started to vibrate across her desk.

What did they want to call the whisky they had worked so hard to create?

Lloyd and Rhona fought over this. A vicious, relentless fight that would stand them in good stead. It wasn't really the name they were fighting about. It was the guilt. Their small act of distilling love had been part of something bigger – the exploitation of what was left of the earth – and they had been wholly complicit.

As they awaited their first tasters, it came to her that she may have been looking to distract them both. After all, distilling and gestation were similar things in some ways. It was all precious liquids and fatty acids stored in specially flavoured barrels.

The night of the phone call, Rhona sat up late breathing in the peat smoke as it burnt cold in front of her. So desperate was she to receive that package from home that, when she tried to sleep, the grouse of her childhood clucked croakily in her ears, preventing her. She could smell the rush of hail on winter heather. She could hear the sploosh of a seal rolling from a rock. Lloyd knew by the way her body moved beside him in the bed that she was crying, but seven years of Rhona had taught him she was visiting a place he could not reach. He rolled over on his side and watched the clock radio tick time away.

Rhona and Lloyd made a silent pact. The joint CEOs never talked about the dram. Both believed the other had stopped waiting for it.

As it always goes, it came when they were least expecting it. Carefully packaged in the artistic box and tissue paper of their own design, Rhona's family name emblazoned across the top of the small wooden parcel.

They got whisky drunk on pride.

Soon after, her periods stopped.

Rhona was playing with the cat when she got the phone call that threatened to pull down their successful company around their ears. Their firm, which they promoted as 'green' and 'community based', was doing so well (they had just moved into the skyscraper business). It would not handle the scandal.

Lying in bed, baby Zaha on his chest, Lloyd heard Rhona shout legal words with unjustified conviction. The new vocabulary of 'environmentally protected' and 'centuries old' and 'peat bog decline' circled the air above him and his daughter like gulls at low tide.

They made the journey to the island.

Now they were three.

Zaha vomited on the ferry. Her uncle Fergus met his niece for the first – and last – time.

At the distillery, they painted the family name off the wall.

Lloyd drove back onto the boat with Zaha in her car seat while Rhona and Fergus said goodbye, their shoulders and knees bent towards each other in the dying light.

The family sailed to the mainland, leaving Port Askraig and Fergus in the dusk. Over a shared bowl of chips on the ferry, Rhona sent a silent apology to her brother.

In a well-practised manner, she registered her emotions and then pushed them from her mind. It was hard not to, with Zaha pushing a chip into her mother's face, her chubby brown hand still learning how to manipulate itself.

Laughing, Rhona picked up her phone to take a picture to send to Fergus and saw the missed call. A call from the Prime Minister's office.

The government had liked their application the most. Their firm would need to be swift in completing their design. They would need to be even speedier in seeing it constructed. Their names would be forever linked to the building of a skyscraper big and bold enough to house an entire city of refugees, fleeing from the almost inevitable environmental chaos that lay ahead. It would put their company on the, albeit potentially quite soggy, map. Did they accept these terms? Would they help to build the first of many Towers?

'We'll call them back as soon as the reception improves,' Rhona suggested.

Lloyd nodded, 'We'll say yes,' he smiled, accepting the chip Zaha was now offering him.

The rest of their journey home was spent in a haze of napkin doodling and excited chatter.

*

Despite being the faces of future town-planning, the now almost-middle-aged architects had always believed that their own eventual escape would be to Rhona's island. They'd head off on the ferry when the evidence spoke more forcefully... When the weathermen stopped showing up for reports... When the rumours of rogue waves and devastating floods became routine, often based in fact... When petrol was becoming scarcer and good solar panels harder to find.

But by the time they'd finished their designs and added the final touches that the officials asked for, riots had spread, like blight on wood, throughout the nation's major towns and cities. Residential streets became the playground of the furious and the scared.

The national transport system began to fall apart. People stopped using it, for fear of attacks led by eco-terrorists. One particular group, who called themselves Gaia's Guys after a series of popular science fiction books, blew up a First Class carriage as it sped out of London King's Cross, killing four newly appointed Ministers for Environmental Affairs. Or, in other words, murdering the fathers of eight children, the boyfriends of two women and a man, and someone's sister.

And so... the ferries no longer sailed. There were no boats to be had.

And, they whispered desperately one night – Zaha sleeping between them – if they did manage to get there, what then? The main road around the island was a quagmire, the airport underwater – or so said the now stranded Fergus.

They wouldn't be able to reach him.

Rhona said, 'I'll only believe it when I see it.'

Lloyd said, 'You get Zaha, I'll get the keys.'

*

They drove the ten hours from London to Kennacraig almost without stopping, Rhona in a fit of pique at all the cars surrounding her on the loch-side roads. Lloyd did the motorway bits, which were, by then, almost as treacherous.

Too late.

'My bad timing,' Rhona growled, as they arrived to find that the spit of land owned by the ferry company had disappeared. A metre further, and their car would have floated away.

In the glow of their headlights, the rain fell sideways, striking glittering holes in the dark water. A wiry tree top was occasionally visible, its mighty trunk submerged beneath the dancing water.

Apart from that, there was no sign of any existence at all.

The weather got madder, things flew across the windscreen of the car. Zaha watched it all silently from her mother's arms. Lloyd scrolled constantly through Twitter, looking for updates about the weather. He kept twisting his face, perpetually worried about rogue waves.

Rhona bit her nails so that they bled on Zaha's Babygro.

Bereft of a plan A, they supported each other against the wind and stumbled out of the car. The rain, now said to carry toxins, landed on their faces, burning cold as it ran down their cheeks.

Then she saw them.

Rhona howled at the sight of over a thousand drowned grouse, floating, bobbing gently against each other, beaks to the sky.

Their bodies stretched far out towards the Sound of Jura.

Sailing to Crouch End

Victoria @mumstheword * 5h
Anyone know what is going on with the rain? #megabeastfromtheEast
#needtogototheshops

Alan @busybody * 5h
@mumstheword it's called climate change love
#keepyourpantson

Victoria @mumstheword * 5h
@busybody seems a bit more than that but thanks for the casual sexism.
What do you think? @weathermanstav #asktheexperts

Alan @busybody * 5h
@mumstheword no problem love and the 'experts' won't give us any
answers

BBC Weather @weathermanstav * 5h
The BBC are sending out advice on the hour, every hour. The
main message from GOV tonight: stay in your homes. If you are
in a prefab or mobile home: seek more stable accommodation.
#BBCreports #staysafecitizens

Victoria @mumstheword * 5h
As I said @busybody, a bit more than nothing to worry about
@weathermanstav, thanks for the #BBCinfo

Marcus @veganandproud * 4h55
typical of the beeb to assume that those in prefabs have somewhere more
'stable' to stay. Anyone in need, if you can get to Crouch End, I've got plenty
of space #everylittlehelps

David @tellitlikeitis * 4h54
@veganandproud, how do you propose we get to Crouch End? Sail?

Poppy @lovemelovemydog * 4h54
Agree with your anger @tellitlikeitis. Tell me @veganandproud, know of
many caravans in the leafy burbs do ya?

Victoria @mumstheword * 4h52
@veganandproud, ignore the trolls. They're probably a
member of #gaiasguys anyway. That was a very kind thing you offered.

Alan @busybody * 4h52
PUT A SOCK IN IT @mumstheword
Bet you're a grouse shooter @veganandproud
#allbankersliveinCrouchEnd

BBC Weather @weathermanstav * 3h
Quick update before I clock off. BBC advice is to stay indoors for
as long as possible. Wind speed is picking up. Red warning for
roads, waterways etc. Emergency services already feeling the strain
#onlyinanemergency #staysafecitizens

BBC Weather @weathermanstav * 3h
Goodnight and good luck

David @tellitlikeitis * 3h
@weathermanstav hope the company car can go underwater

Poppy @lovemelovemydog * 3h
@weathermanstav what does the BBC suggest I do with
my three bulldogs who are all bursting for a peepee?
#idcallthisanemergency

Victoria @mumstheword * 2h30
@GOVUK any advice on what to do if water gets in?

Alan @busybody * 2h29
@mumstheword go upstairs you ninny. Or go stay with @veganandproud

Victoria @mumstheword * 2h24
@busybody, thanks Alan but for real @GOVUK it's coming in really
quickly and I've got two young boys

UK Citizens Advice @GOVUK * 2h
Please stay inside your homes. Shut all the windows and doors. If any water or mist comes into contact with skin, shower immediately.

Marcus @veganandproud * 2h
@mumstheword how are the boys? Did you get any water on you? Read the guidelines here on the gov.co.uk website.

Alan @busybody * 1h55
love is in the air @mumstheword @veganandproud

Poppy @lovemelovemydog * 1h54
Is that what is in the mist/water @GOVUK? Love?
#labourcanclearupthedogpissbehindmysofa

UK Citizens Advice @GOVUK * 1h50
The rainwater is highly toxic. Stay in your homes until you are rescued by air. Rescues will take place in the areas of most flooding first of all. Track your nearest air-ambulance here gov.co.uk

Marcus @veganandproud * 1h49
@mumstheword where's your nearest air-ambulance?

David @tellitlikeitis * 1h48
@veganandproud it'll not be anywhere north of the M25!

Alan @busybody * 1h30
@mumstheword have you found one Victoria? Let us know what the travel conditions are like. Hopefully better than @LNER services, right @tellitlikeitis? #wecan'talltravelfirstclass

David @tellitlikeitis * 1h30
@busybody you're damned right my man!
#nationalisetherailways

Marcus @veganandproud * 1h25
@mumstheword any news?

Poppy @lovemelovemydog * 1h21
@mumstheword @veganandproud agreed – what's happening?

Marcus @veganandproud * 55m
@GOVUK what should we do if a friend is trapped? @mumstheword

Alan @busybody * 52m
@GOVUK hate to agree with @veganandproud but it has been over 2
hours since we last heard from @mumstheword

David @tellitlikeitis * 50m
@busybody the rain has reached mine now, so keep those windows
shut

Alan @busybody * 49m
thanks @tellitlikeitis, already on it bud.
@veganandproud – Marcus, any news on @mumstheword?

Marcus @veganandproud * 46m
@busybody no luck mate @GOVUK there is nothing on
the TV nothing on the radio etc What on earth is going on?
#wedeserveanswers

Poppy @lovemelovemydog * 30m
@veganandproud @GOVUK website has crashed.
#5Gwouldhavecomeinhandy

Alan @busybody * 25m
@tellitlikeitis @veganandproud @mumstheword
@lovemelovemydog we're on our own fellas
#BrexitBritain

David @tellitlikeitis * 24m
@busybody nice knowing ya, bud

Alan @busybody * 23m
@tellitlikeitis likewise fella

Marcus @veganandproud * 23m
@mumstheword @lovemelovemydog @tellitlikeitis @busybody helicopter in area, will keep you posted #letssticktogether

Alan @busybody * 22m
@veganandproud typical, save the bankers first #IdRatherDrown

David @tellitlikeitis * 21m
@veganandproud enjoy the ride #Londonfirst

Poppy @lovemelovemydog * 15m
@tellitlikeitis @busybody just us three now (and the pooches of course) #allyouneedisdogs

Alan @busybody * 15m
@lovemelovemydog let's hope they can swim!

David @tellitlikeitis * 14m
@lovemelovemydog and that you don't run out of food!

Alan @busybody * 10m
@tellitlikeitis looks like it is just us two now David #cheerstothat

David @tellitlikeitis * 9m
@busybody chin up Alan pal!

UK Citizens Advice @GOVUK * 5m
Floods and high winds disrupting the power grids. Charge phones and other electronic devices for as long as you can. Refrain from any activity that uses a lot of energy. Red weather warnings across country. Stay inside. #staysafecitizens

Alan @busybody * 4m
@tellitlikeitis here it goes then dude. Do not go quietly and all that

David @tellitlikeitis * 4m
@busybody oh I'm raging I assure you #staysafecitizensmyarse

UK Citizens Advice @GOVUK * 1m
According to meteorologists there is now a high chance of freak waves off
eastern coastal areas. If you need to move to higher land, please do so. Cover
as much of your skin as possible. #staysafecitizens

BBC @worldservice * just now
Slight delay to broadcasting. Keep your radios tuned.

Messages:

Director @GeneralD Jul 7
Time to switch it all off now, team. Thank you for your incredible service
tonight, and over the years.
It has been an honour.

Middle

2032

Up on the Roof (At Noon)

The alarm rings at quarter to, work starts at noon. At noon, the winds are at their strongest and the sun at its highest although that would be hard to tell. Up on the roof, the cloud is so thick, you can almost eat it.

It has been a year and a half since I have seen blue sky.

It is an uncomfortable feeling, being shrouded in clouds. The sky seems heavier than the ground. Gravity seems confused too, and the ground trembles every other day or so. Just as I predicted in my research, the mantle of the earth is trying its damnedest to shake us off, and into the clouds.

I don't blame it.

I roll out of my cot. Standing too quickly, I bang my head. The narrow rooms that I bargained and bartered my knowledge and soul for are as oppressive as the clouds.

The plaster smells constantly of damp. I've learnt it is best to put my uniform on last thing, so as to keep the dank smell at bay.

I have time to spare. I close my eyes against the grey hum of the single energy-saving bulb, it does funny things to my vision. I often see shadows when trying to sleep, I can almost make out words scrawled beneath the ever-damp paint above my cot.

Sometimes, I consider adding to the historic document, but I don't know where there are any pens. Also, I have more or less forgotten how to write.

And what would I say?

*

Before Everything Went Wrong, time to spare was a luxury. Five minutes meant a status update, a new follower on Twitter, a few picture-flicks to spy on friends or past lovers. A chat with a parent, a quickly scribbled birthday card.

Now there are no phones. No one I know. No parents. No birthdays.

I decide to be early. Maybe whoever cares about these things will notice. Maybe I'll be promoted. To what, I'm not sure. Unless you're a Scientist, all uniforms are the same, so the hierarchy is still unclear to me. Perhaps this is because it needs to be. I hate that I still feel a need to please. I used to be a scientist, but I have outlived my usefulness, it seems.

Five to. My cubicle door shuts slowly behind me. I start to climb the twelve flights to the roof.

I make myself recount what was before. It does get easier, the more I relive the moments.

A moment for every flight of stair:

One: Snatches of blue sky in a summer heatwave, some years ago. Snatches of headlines predicting environmental doom.

Two: Our dogs panting heavily, overheating. September, October – too warm for coats when we walked them in November. Too wet for short sleeves.

Three: Dogs starving now, bones sticking out everywhere. No reason, said the vet – perhaps something in their food? Something in the air?

I wipe some sweat from my cheek. Where is that vet now?

Four: Unnatural, midday darkness. Heavy clouds. Silent birds. Silent people, hurrying in the streets. Supermarkets empty of the milk that was already starting to taste sour.

Here, there isn't food, as such, just nutrient mulch. It is a similar colour to the walls and the clouds. A pallid margin laps at everything here. It is not as tragic as you might think, even if you glance out the windows. It is reassuring, almost, that there is nothing outside to see.

Five: Sleeping with the bedroom windows open on Christmas Eve – the rain hammering onto concrete outside, sheets sticking to us in the heat.

I lick some sweat from my top lip and keep a steady pace. Climbing up and up.

Six: New Year's Day – the dead birds all over the ground. The moans as the smell began to rise.

I am almost at the roof now. Almost ready to keep watch.

Seven: Heavy, burning rain striking us as we moved to the Tower. Or were moved. People in masks, hazmat suits. Silent. Unforgivingly uninformative. Holding guns.

Guns like the one I hold when I stand on duty.

Eight: The sadness of the holding cells. Beds everywhere, bodies supine, eyes glued to the grey ceiling.

Nine: The protection of the Tower. The comforting whir of the air conditioning. A whine of irony at its continued use, even at the planet's end.

Two minutes to go and I am at the door to the roof. I lean against it for just a moment. It is difficult for me to catch my breath these days.

Ten: The questions that haunted the waking minutes. Where are the dogs now? Are they alive? Is the house on fire, looted? Gone? Hushed conversations between beds, and the dawning realisation that everything we once knew had been twisted. All had been heated and cooled, and was now unrecognisable.

Eleven: Your hand, when it stopped squeezing.

Twelve: Stepping out alone when they opened the cell. Climbing up to my quarters. Alone, in the Tower. The new, grey sky.

I hurl myself against the door and fall out onto the roof. High railings loom over me. Feeling dizzy, I crouch for a moment, letting this depleted world spin around me.

I wipe my cheek again and shoulder my gun. I stand, I look up – hoping to see a flying shape amongst the clouds.

I gasp.

It is noon.

The sky is blue.

The Greenhouse

When I shut my eyes, I can see it all.

There was a vast field, its sky-line all higgledy-piggledy with sheds, lean-tos and apple trees. There was a gate that creaked with overuse when I unlocked it. A row of plots spilled out in front of me. They looked a mess at a distance, but order was restored as I walked among them. Some plots had names, some numbers. There were even occasional flags, underlining horticultural love stories in happy rainbow colours or bold prints.

At one edge of our plot stood the small, but surprisingly spacious, greenhouse. It was the only greenhouse in the whole place that had green paint on its metal fixtures. It was not the same old white, metal and glass greenhouse that we saw, on repeat, as we walked to plot 25. Our plot stood out, due to this simple choice of colour.

Inside the greenhouse, tomato plants grew proud. Watered by an irrigation system of clandestine tubes and pipes. A timer set to tell it when to recycle the plentiful rainwater from the gutter. I can still conjure up the fruit's acid-smell – at once delicately sharp and earthily hearty. It was a generous jungle, the glass silencing the outside world for a little while and making the warm space so quiet, we sometimes heard a tomato drop.

I am sure that my memory hasn't made it any more beautiful than it really was. Simple and beautiful. That was you all over.

*

But that was then. Now, life revolves around a different Greenhouse. It sits high up, at the very top of the Tower in which we all live. Its door is the only way in and out of the whole complex (that I know of). Between the door to the Greenhouse and the door leading to the stairs back down to our quarters there is a small space. It is only big enough for one human at a time. This space is covered by a cage of tight metal bars, just in case. In the gaps between the metal, I can taste the heavy clouds pressing in.

Inside, we work in silence. It is hard to remember if this is because we're being watched or because we have nothing to say. Strangers to each other.

Alone in our worlds of potato lifting or seed-sowing or herb hybridising. Sweat drips onto the plants. The vast, glass space is tangy with body odour, heavy with nothing but the breathing of the overexerted and under-fed.

Theft reduces rations, we know.

*

61

When we first rented the plot, it was a mess. My dreams of a first-year glut of hefty aubergines and popping-fresh peas were quickly crushed under the weight of all that weeding. And cutting. And hacking back. And pulling. And aching. And sleeping more soundly than either of us had ever slept, our hands clasped under the duvet, that magic earth still under the odd fingernail. Your arm still flecked with green paint.

We spent evenings on deckchairs by a freshly dug bed, drinking beer in the last of the September sun. I would wrap up and sit there with my notebook, my constant companion, writing it all down. Trying to get the final book written.

Before the clouds rolled in.

We started to say things that we heard the other allotmenteers say:

'Great to be on a hill, lots of drainage.'

and

'Oh, it'll be a tough autumn for brassicas.'

and

'When did the manure man say he'd get here?'

*

When we first got here, the world we left was in such a mess that our small quarters seemed a blessing. The day they airlifted us away, you stopped my tears with your sleeve. Said we were lucky to be part of the lottery. My knuckles, tight around your arm, strained to burst their skin as we went up. As they brought us, the lottery winners, here.

We spent the first few months getting our bearings, overcoming altitude sickness, getting used to our blue uniforms, finding out which plants might grow. We were allocated separate shifts, but shared the same room. Although I missed my books and my desk, and you missed your kitchen, we started to settle in, to say things that we heard the other workers say:

'Could be worse, we could still be down there.'

and

'Lots of jobs, so we'll be keeping busy.'

and

'What happened to our homes?'

*

But then, we got the hang of it. And suddenly, we had a plethora of courgettes and carrots, corn and kohlrabi. We had strawberries coming out of our ears and rhubarb as high as our knees. Your recipes lengthened. We netted and weeded and split and transplanted with the best of the 'allotmenteers'. We almost won an award. Our world went from: Traffic – Work – Bills – Plumbers

To: Life – The sustaining of life – The creation of more life – The supporting of life.

But then, they split us up. Two women can't create life, they argued. And suddenly, there is no team. And now, life is less green, despite many days up here in the Greenhouse, surrounded by potato-lifters, seed-sowers or herb-hybridisers. My shift never matches your shift. My path never crosses yours. My world has gone from: You – Us

To: Just me.

*

My favourite plants on our plot were the fruit bushes. They looked messy, even when tended to. They stuck out in odd places. Yet – even the least hopeful dark stem bore ripe, red fruit. They were always ready for our arrival, happy to share their sharp berry wealth.

Your favourite plant, if I remember correctly, were the sprouts.

'They taste even better if there is a really bad frost,' you told me once, glancing up from your preferred gardening book. 'How clever is that?'

*

My favourite plants in the Greenhouse are the potatoes. They produce pretty flowers. They don't know or care that flowers are surplus to requirements up here. They bloom in spite of the rules, cheery against the gloomy grey skies.

Your favourite plant is unknown to me now. I imagine you like the section full of medicinal herbs and curative stems. Lavenders grow so high there that you can get lost in them. Every now and then the smell drifts across to the patch where I work.

'The smell of lavender stays in your hair for ages,' you told me once, breathing in deeply as we lay together on the sofa, after another long day of maintaining our dream. 'How delicious is that?'

*

We held a party to celebrate me finishing the last book in the series and, of course, to show off our green-fingered success. We wondered how many more parties we would be able to throw.

We wore wild flowers from our patch in our hair and button holes. We filled jugs with verdant leaves and toasted the allotment and its greenhouse with home-made rhubarb gin, red-berry cordial and Blackberry Royales. At the centre of the table was a carved pumpkin lantern. When the generator stopped working (solar power only got us so far and we had been using the oven too much), the lantern kept our faces bathed in a warm glow.

Later that evening, as we sat around groaning about how full we were (your magic food: cauliflower cheese, new potatoes, pan-seared broccoli, sautéed carrots), the pumpkin lid caught fire from the candle underneath. We fell about laughing at our drunken attempts to put it out.

One day a week, there is a meeting for each section. A government official sits before us and gives information, answers questions. I am not in your section. You are not in mine. I never see you at the meetings. I only go in the hope that I will. And to make contact with the rest of us. We all make an effort with our hair on these days. We all have a wild look in our eyes. We speak too loudly, because we can't remember how to speak normally.

One day a week, news arrives. The names of those who have been rescued, where they have been sent. Data concerning rainfall, where the latest wave has hit.

We ask questions, but receive no answers. As the meeting wears on, the murmuring of unanswered questions rises (Where is she? Where is he? Where are they?)

*

I used to struggle with the bugs on our plot – especially the courgette spiders. Crooked and spiky, they were unnervingly fast. It seemed that the more I tried to avoid them, the more they sought me out.

'They run towards me!' I squealed at you as you laughed, leaning on the spade in the light drizzle.

You struggled with the work – especially the digging. You slowed down quickly, looking tired. It seemed that the more you stuck your spade in, the smaller you became.

'I'm not built for this,' you reminded me, as we heaved at an old root-ball together, trying to remove it from the ground.

*

I miss the outdoors. I linger too long in the cage that leads out from the Greenhouse. I breathe in the cooling cloud, wonder how high up I am, try to look over the edge. I stare down into the grey fog below. The expanse is hypnotising and appealing, reaching up towards me. Someone, perhaps worried to see me fixating on the edge, touches my arm and guides me away.

Do you struggle with the work? Are you, like me, working in the Greenhouse? Or maybe the kitchen, or a laundry room?

'I'm not built for this,' you warn me at night, when I imagine you into being, trying to hold your delicate face vivid in my mind.

*

When the rain didn't stop for a fortnight, we were both at a loss. We raincoated-up. Wellies on, we stood in our plot, trying not to sink in the mud. I couldn't tell if you were crying, like I was, or if it was the rain on your cheeks.

You cracked a joke about the rain being a useful resource for hydropower, but you didn't smile.

The only things that would survive were the tomatoes, the seedlings, the cacti. Secure and dry in the greenhouse, the one you painted with green touches. Standing safe inside, it felt as though we had front row seats for the end of the world. We tried not to steam the glass up with our breath.

*

These days, the rain doesn't go on for so long. We don't need raincoats they gave us, or wellies; our uniforms are sufficient. Once, when we'd first arrived, I stood in the cage long enough to be rained on. It felt nice. I can't tell if I miss the rain, or if it is just me missing you.

The only things that will survive this are our bodies, our gripping hands and our strong thighs. Secure and alive in the Greenhouse, the kitchens, the laundry rooms – wherever you now work. We will grow outwardly and cultivate privately.

*

Only the tallest grasses could be seen. Only the top few panes of our greenhouse, on the edge of the plot. In our hands, we cradled the last few pods and leaves we could salvage. They were mushy, waterlogged, tasteless.

The rain kept falling. Where once stood a variety of beloved plots, there was now a lake, a glorified puddle. Near to us, but apart, stood other allotment-owners, clutching remnants in their hands.

'We can start again, when the water level falls,' you spoke softly and put your head on my shoulder.

*

The first harvest is remarkable. Remarkable enough to warrant a demand for workers from other sections. I don't know this until I arrive in the cage. It is a truly vertiginous feeling, being so high up.

Seeing you, in overalls just like mine, your hair pulled up high – yet to be shaved off – almost sends me over the edge.

You don't stop digging. There is a sea of workers between us. We are near, but apart.

'We can start again,' I want to shout to you, as I watch you struggle with the digging, 'when the water level falls.'

You look over your shoulder, as if you hear me. When you see me, a smile unfurls on your face. It is a smile of hope, shooting up, spring-green.

Green – like the paint on the metal fixtures of our little greenhouse, the one that used to stand proud on the edge of our small plot.

65

Accidental Flowers

'Were you a chef, before you got here?' Her accent introduces me to misted hills and heather, carrying on its lilt the burnt-tyre smell of a good Scotch. She drags a chair from the table to the concrete counter-top where I work. It scuds along the floor, metal feet on zinc flooring. When she sits down, I can feel her breath, warm on my elbow.

'I don't know.' I don't look at her. I look backwards, but I can't remember. When I try to, all I see is a shelf loaded with cookbooks. A pair of oven gloves and a window with a view of neat, parcelled allotments that is almost blocked by a pot, full of kitchen contraptions. A mantelpiece with a row of trophies and plaques. My face on the back of a packet of something – pasta maybe?

And then I look forward and here I am in this sorry excuse for a kitchen. There is no bridge of memory between the two. Nothing to transport us over the water that now surrounds this building, this world. Just the quiet but distinct sound of waves.

Don't dwell. I chop roughly at the herb in front of me. You must get this right.

'Good,' she seems satisfied, but there is caution in her voice and a hint of challenge. I can still feel her eyes on me. 'Neither do I. I think I was an architect.'

The herb is an attempt at rosemary. It has the right sort of leaves, but when chopped, they release a spiciness that makes me think of curry. I offer her my fingers, covered in the plant's juices, 'Does this smell like curry to you?'

She sniffs, looking up at me with heavy eyelids, as if from underwater. She nods.

'I'd murder a Biryani.'

I laugh slightly, gathering the leaves together. With no recipe book, little memory of any recipes or any real idea of what produce we have here, even I don't know what I'm doing.

'Do you have any Mediterranean-type herbs up there?' I nod my head at the ceiling, visualising the Greenhouses twenty storeys above us, greenhouses that I've been banned from, for the time being. Due to my 'hysteria', apparently. That wonderful day when I think – no, I am sure – that I saw Colleen. It will be a while until I'm allowed the same multi-storey access again. The increased freedom you get as a reward. 'Freedom' that I will be granted, if I get this right. She tells me I am silly to be excited, that there isn't much up there, but I can already taste the mulch on my tongue. I can see the almost-potatoes, the hybridised onions. And maybe, some accidental flowers, growing where nobody's looking.

She shrugs. 'No idea, sorry. I don't work upstairs because of my horticultural talent, you know. It is just where I was put. I think.'

I sigh, irritation and a small dollop of burning panic unwelcome in my voice, 'I mean… anything that looks like it would belong on a pizza, or in a pasta dish or–'

She laughs through her nose. 'You get really irritated when I don't take cooking seriously.'

I hate the word cooking. It sticks in my throat like jam in a jar where the knife can't reach. 'I'm not cooking!' I want to shout right into her delicate face. 'I'm creating!'

I don't, because compared to my normal daily existence, cooking is luxury incarnate. To be in a kitchen and not cleaning toilets, to wear an apron – and I must not mess this up.

'The Mediterranean…' she plays with the word on her tongue. 'Didn't people used to go there on cheap holidays? Sunbathe, paddle in the s–'

'I just…' I stare down at the herb, bleeding green on the board. 'I have to take this task seriously.' So that they take me seriously.

She nods, 'That's true.' She nibbles a bit of the rosemary-curry leaf. 'Don't we all…' Her eyebrows cut into her nose and she spits into her hand. 'Man, is that bitter!'

I shake my head. How can I work without the proper ingredients? There are rumours on our storey about contraband, but they are just too delicious sounding to believe.

She stands up, reaching her arms above her head in a stretch that allows me a small glimpse of round hips and the line of softly-downed stomach above her blue uniform. All the Greenhouse work, delivering, climbing the stairs – it must keep her really strong.

Keep on task.

'What is this stuff even made of?' She moves around so that she is opposite me. She takes a spoon and pokes at the pink lump that sits in the centre of the counter-top. It wobbles.

'They told me,' I swallow, 'and I'm trying so hard to remember.'

She touches my knife hand. She looks me right in the eye. 'Don't try too hard,' she warns. 'Remember how it all disappears if you look straight at it.'

We both nod. I can feel the waves lapping at the edges of my mind. I squeeze her hand with my free finger and thumb. She returns the favour, then detaches.

I resume chopping, every nerve ending in my hand shooting fireworks up my arm.

'I think they grew it in one of their labs,' I say, after a moment.

I put the knife down. We look at the block of 'meat'. It glistens pinkly. It is like an opaque jelly. It makes me think of blancmange, if blancmange had the ridged quality of frozen mince. She leans down and sniffs it. Her nose wrinkles up at me.

'Weirdly sweet, isn't it?' I say.

She agrees. 'It's almost like it's off.'

She prods it again. A ripple goes through it. She shudders. 'Now I understand why people used to choose to be vegetarian.'

There's no choice here. We eat what we can grow, in those Greenhouses high above us. Everything comes ready-salted by the oceans, encroaching below us. Oceans empty of life, they tell us. Although I'm sure that is scientifically impossible. Just not sure enough to argue. There was a rumour, a few months ago, of a fishing excursion going wrong, but the details are vague to me now. But people need balanced diets and so they've come up with this… lump of meat, this rose-tinged slab, this–

'Extracellular Matrix!' I cry, victorious. 'That's what they called it!'

'Well remembered!' She pushes a stray hair from her forehead, eyebrows once again crinkled. 'But do you think I can eat it raw?'

I shrug. My shoulders ache. The counter is too low. When I put my hands on it, I have to bend. There was once a counter measured exactly to my height, complete with a forest of herbs beneath a canopy of pots and pans. I can remember the smells of seared meat, creamy fish and–

'Don't go back there,' she warns, 'unless it is going to help you with your task.'

Her words part the sea, hold the tsunami at bay.

Listen to her. I push the herbs to one side and pick up a withered and brown bulb-like object.

'Is this meant to be garlic?'

Her smile reveals the tip of her tongue. 'Yes.' Then she points at the herb, 'Just like that is meant to be rosemary.'

I roll my eyes, start peeling the root. The tang of almost-garlic fills the small, white space. The cloves are brown, but not soft, not rotten. I swallow down hope-laced saliva at the bulb's delicious scent. I begin to chop finely, breathing in deeply.

'That smell is making me hungry,' her voice is low, a thrum of anticipation. 'How long 'til we can try… it?'

The garlic chopped, I turn to the collection of proteins. I can feel Them watching me, from somewhere else inside the building. With a deep breath, I pick it up. It slips from my fingers and lands back on its plate.

'Did that thing just squelch?' She asks, playing with a leftover sprig of rosemary.

I try again. My gripping nails sink into the mass and a bit of it begins to peel away. I let it fall back down.

I pick up my knife. As I slice the protein, it meets no resistance. No ripping of flesh, no expected suggestion of fat. A hot knife through butter. The smell catches in my throat.

She is transfixed, watching me work. She sits like somebody in my memory, a smaller somebody, watching my hands with glee, singing a song about chopping and taking a scrap of something I am offer–

'Look at your nails!'

They have turned bright pink and are red-rimmed.

'Don't worry.' She notices my fingers trembling. 'Let's just get it done.'

I nod, grab the pan, turn on the electric hob. There is a hum as somewhere, a generator ramps up some energy.

When the small amount of oil (corn, I think) that they provided is hot, I throw in the protein, expecting at least a sizzle. There is no sound. We lean in over the pan, straining to hear something delicious, a suggestion that I've done something right.

Steam rises. A sweet smell enters our noses, trickles into our throats. I cough. I move away from the pan, unable to stop spluttering. My nose streams. My lungs fill. I turn on the ventilator above the oven and look around for a non-existent window. They don't like windows in the kitchens, and they'd never have one you can open. Too risky.

I move towards the door.

'No!' She shouts from the corner, her hand over her nose. 'Someone will complain; and they'll make us leave before it's ready.'

I run back over to the pan and place a lid on top.

She joins me.

'Let's hope it tastes better than it smells.' She puts a hand on my shoulder and wipes a tear from the corner of my eye. I shake my head. *Don't be scared.*

'If it doesn't work, you know what will happen. You know that They'll…'

She covers my mouth with a smooth, cool hand. The hand that, just a minute ago, had protected her from the protein fumes. The water recedes once again.

'You won't fail. Think of the Greenhouses, think of the outs–' I shake my head. There is snot from my nose on her hand, but she doesn't remove it. 'Tomatoes! Don't forget the tomatoes I brought.' Her voice is low, her mouth close to my ear.

I nod. Slowly, she removes her hand.

The tomatoes are the shape of pears. Their cool weight in my hand makes me think of the first puddings of autumn, of ginger peel and cinnamon. Their skins are almost purple, the colour of dried blood. The fruit clashes horribly with my pink fingernails.

Again, I get to work. I can feel their eyes on me, I try to picture their satisfied nods as I continue my task of chopping and occasionally stopping to check that all the meat is sealed.

When I've chopped enough, I add all the ingredients to the pan. She looks at me, once again, with a wonder that makes me think of another somebody, with eyes too big for their face under their crown of hair, held back with a brightly coloured ba–

'Hey, is it ready to go in the oven?' She is shaking her head slowly at me.

Don't think, just do.

A tap drips into the sink behind her.

'Almost. Just have to add this,' I pick up a glass bottle full of the thick brown liquid we drink for breakfast here.

'Urgh!' She rolls her eyes. 'Why do you have to put that in?'

'It is sort of like stock, isn't it?'

She grins. 'Just like the rosemary is sort of like rosemary.'

'And the garlic is almost garlic,' I agree.

Her laughter bounces about the kitchen before wrapping me up tightly. It is infectious. I'm still smiling as I pour in some of our food-fuel and put the lid back on. Still grinning as I slide the concoction into the oven. There is still a light in both of our eyes when one of the government officials comes in to ask how long it will be, to check progress, and to send us back to our separate quarters until it's ready to be tasted.

To Whom It May Concern

I bang a pair of metal bowls together. Instant barking, birds screaming out of the bank of trees to my right. The ground rumbles with the approach of an army, a flood, a crush of hungry mongrels. Slavering, yipping, tails wagging with sheer anticipation. I put each portion of oats and vegetables out in a line. They're used to it now – each one finds their favoured bowl, and doesn't bother the others. Today, I count fifteen. Two fewer than yesterday.

I hope they've found somewhere better, where the rabbits are more plentiful. I can't help but smile at the pack, a line of waggling bottoms, wolfing down their food. The skin around my cheek stretches, tight with yesterday's unexpected sun. I think I may have burnt myself. I make a mental note to add moisturiser to the loot-list.

Since day one, I've been pleasantly surprised at how the dogs have managed to remain in the unscathed condition in which they turned up. The oats are keeping their coats – once domesticated and glossy – in a good enough state. They are yet to be truly wild, memories of warm sofas and homemade peanut-butter treats still linger. And judging by their collective heft, the majority of them must still be getting meat from somewhere. They're too robust to be living out here purely on the mush we put aside for them.

My favourite is a short brown mongrel, who, due to her own personal odyssey, I have called Argos (technically, she's a bitch, but technically, so am I). She cleans her bowl thoroughly, chasing it around the dewy grass with her tongue. When she's finished, she looks up, finally notices me. She moves to nuzzle the hand that fed her. Her behaviour tells me that she must have been the love of a small child's life, before. Her ears are still so soft, despite two long years of feral living. I feel my cheeks and wish I could claim the same.

I drop down onto my haunches and she sniffs at my ear. My laugh makes a nearby terrier stop eating to look at me. With a satisfied grunt, Argos trots behind me and into the door of my cabin (a glorified shed).

So, maybe she is less feral than the others. Perhaps she is used to sharing my cabin with me, on the colder nights. She's my own personal alarm clock, really. On some winter mornings, it is quite useful to have her warmth and rhythm beside me – especially since Martha is totally anti-electricity.

Like yesterday, today is going to be warm. The cloud is already thinning, burning off. I can see blue. Soon, the sun – all the light we need – will move around the Tower and chase away its own long shadow.

I'd better get on with the human breakfast, before the other four wake.

*

Human breakfast is its usual cacophony of yawns and stretched-sighs. Hair is more mussed than usual, eyes blearier. Graham's nose is red from the homebrew, Aleks and Martha are still wound around each other like climbing beans around a wigwam. Troy is still too tired to radiate envy towards them. We sit, blankets on our shoulders, around the fire. We have nothing to say to each other. The working day has yet to begin. I watch the Tower's shadow, falling across my cabin and Graham's, change and shift with the movement of the sun. The odd dog comes over to sniff at our half-empty bowls, but is quickly shooed away. We do try to keep some sort of perimeter around our 'kitchen' – otherwise everything starts to smell of piss. Argos, by far the cleverest, lies just inside the door of my cabin, sniffing the air and awaiting the small warm patch the sun will soon provide.

When we're sated, our postures change. We lengthen in the sun, chests out, breathing calm. We wait in silence for Martha to take out the list from the backpack she always keeps attached to the handles of her wheelchair. We look away as she shrugs off Aleks, who folds in on himself, his head on his hands, his hoodie patched and loose. I'll look for another one, on my next trip out of camp. That might cheer him up. Give us the pleasant surprise of a smile on his face.

'Right.' Martha's voice is scratchy with hay fever, even though she swears she doesn't suffer from it, that these things don't exist in the new world. They do. Just like periods exist and desire exists and sciatica exists, hay fever exists. Below-the-waist paralysis exists.

None of us know what happened to Martha. We are not allowed to ask. Despite all her rules and beliefs, it is the same world; our bodies are the same bodies. Well… almost the same. Parts of my body, bound beneath layers of material, are separate to me now. Who I was, she is an old friend from the past. I love her dearly, but she is not me now. In all the upheaval, I left her behind.

'Robin, are you listening?' Martha swims back into focus. I nod.

'We've got to complete an outstanding order.'

Graham – 'Today? I thought we weren't going to work today!'

Troy, laughing at his friend, who he knew from Before, – 'Regretting all the hooch, Gray?'

'You're damned right, I have a pre-holiday hangover.'

'Hangovers don't exist,' says Martha, in a voice that suggests that she is used to being in charge. 'Shake it off.'

Graham says nothing, just narrows his light eyes above ruddy, stubbled cheeks.

'It will only take two of us.' Martha's serenity would have pissed me off before. When I first stumbled into the camp, she drove me crazy with her rules and beliefs. She is such a zealot, muttering late into the night about the horrible fate that should befall petrol companies and energy providers, but then I saw everything she did for us and well – we'd be absolutely screwed without her. Sure, she can't do the heavy lifting, but what's physical power without knowledge? Now I accept that if I want to stay, Martha is part of the deal.

'Robin, Troy?'

Troy shrugs. I shrug, trying to hide my increased heart rate. I look at Aleks looking at Martha looking at Troy and, as expected, I see a slow smile spread across his face. Happy boy, he can stay back with his Martha.

'Gray, Aleks – will you help me set up for later?'

We're celebrating today. This is our first 'party', but we don't really know what to call it. It is a birthday, in some ways. It is the birth of us, the camp, the new start. The day the five of us first sat down and drew up our charter, our rules.

It has been a year (give or take a few days) since the Tower shut its doors.

So, it is also a wake.

Or – better yet – a memorial.

*

'You can bring her, whatever.' Troy nods at Argos, who is standing at the door to my cabin with that look in her eyes. The whole world at her paws, yet she still needs a human to tell her when it is time to go for a walk. I tap my leg and she jumps into step with us as we head out. Troy waves lazily at the others who are busy party-planning over a second cup of coffee.

I sniff the air. 'Cheeky bastards, they're using that good Waitrose stuff we took.'

Troy sniffs too. His proud face in repose reminds me of the faces on the front covers of the magazines I used to buy when I was a teenager. He shrugs. 'I packed us some supplies, don't worry.'

We make our way down the hill to the warehouses and the library. They stand, squat but fresh, in what was once three connected allotment plots. Graham, our in-house Architect/Builder, calls them his 'proudest achievement'. He claims he used to work at the firm that came up with the idea and design for the Towers and that their work parties were raucous… but that is about all the personal information we got from him.

The Tower seems to loom so close it feels like it might topple over onto us, even though really, we're no nearer than we were up at camp. Troy and I look up for a moment, eyes tracing the trunk of the great metal tree until it goes missing in the sky. Not being able to see where it ends makes me dizzy. It just…

disappears, piercing through the cloud like a knife through the skin on over-boiled milk. I drop to my haunches, before the ground comes up to meet me. Argos whines slightly.

'You okay Rob?'

Deep down, underneath all my layers of binding, I know I am in love with Troy. We found him on my first exploration away from Martha's camp. He was curled on top of some cardboard on an old raised bed, a half-bag of compost as a pillow. Eyes wide-open, blinking up at the sky.

He was the only one to take my reinvention at face value. He calls me Rob, treats me just the same as he treats Aleks and Graham. Well, almost.

Troy doesn't question, he is not interested in what was before. Hidden is as hidden does. He looks towards the future with his strong nose and full lips and his beautiful face has the power to make us all want to see what he sees there.

Troy takes out the list and looks at me –

'Library first?'

I nod.

The library is the only warehouse built of metal. Martha seemed to think that would protect the books more. The waves of corrugated iron remind me of the spines of books. It is quite fitting.

The door complains as I pull it open, screeching across the flag-stone floor. Inside everything smells like mushrooms. The floor is a pattern of cardboard boxes, propped up on bricks, with genres scrawled on the outside.

'Yet another order for… and I quote … "anything from the *Goodbye to Gaia* series".'

'They're so popular.' I head to a box labelled sci-fi/fantasy.

I sort through. Some of the covers stick to my hand with moisture.

'Who is the author again?'

'Nkosi,' Troy answers. 'Colleen Nkosi.'

'Ah, that's it!' I say, as I strike gold and pull out two hefty tomes: *Crisis* and *The Seeds Won't Grow.*

I show them to Troy. He nods.

'She wrote that one about this allotment. Theirs was next to ours,' he says, nodding at *The Seeds Won't Grow.*

New information, willingly divulged! I try to keep my excitement under wraps. I crouch, silent, my face passive, hoping he'll tell me more.

He coughs, looks back at his list.

'Next… five bottles of wine – red,' he laughs through his nose. 'A "selection" apparently. Can just imagine the person who asked for this.'

Argos barks at nothing in particular. I wonder if her owners were used to wine deliveries. She must have come from one of the houses near our allotments, so perhaps hers was a house we looted. Maybe we're just returning the bottles to their original owners. Argos barks again, as if confirming my thoughts. I ruffle her ears, stand back up.

'I'll get those. Anything else from warehouse one?'

Troy runs an earthy thumb down the list and then nods. 'Four bottles of gin,' he laughs. 'The litre ones. Someone up there is planning a fiesta!'

We exit the library. I lock it and Troy makes sure the door is secure.

I head over to the bottle warehouse and unlock. Inside it is dark and smells of pine. I imagine the sound of liquid sloshing in the rows of bottles that greet me.

We have taken our 'produce' from all over town. Amazing, the stuff that people panic bought or looted or kept back before it all went down. Amazing that it is now finding its way back to them. And to us too.

'Maybe sneak in a bottle of whisky for later?' Troy shouts from warehouse two (chocolate, biscuits, various confectionery with long use-by dates, toothpaste, shampoo, perfume, contraceptives). Argos barks at him in response as I slip a bottle into my backpack along with a few bottles of the wine and gin. Troy will have to haul the rest. I think of his arms full. Some sweat dances along my hairline. Argos whines at the door to the warehouse. Onward. I lug my load outside. Troy and I divide everything between us before setting out on the, by now, well worn path to the Tower.

*

Our journey takes us out of the gate to the north of the allotments. We connect with the central motorway and then follow its barely noticeable slope all the way down to the Tower. It is roughly three miles, but with all the bottles, it feels longer. Of course, it would be much faster in a car, but transport that requires fuel of any kind other than human effort is banned. Martha's world, Martha's rules.

And anyway, petrol supplies are drying up – I can't remember the last time I saw a car pass this way.

Even though it is only spring, I start to sweat quickly – it is to be expected with all the layers going on beneath my t-shirt. Troy's slight sheen is nothing on my flood. I can taste salt at the back of my throat.

'It is a good day for our party,' Troy comments, after a few minutes of silence.

'Talking about the weather,' I laugh. 'Some things don't change,'

The Tower stands resolute in front of us. It is easy, the closer you get, to convince yourself that there are people at the windows. That you can see the shapes of faces. Shadowed movements. We know it to be a trick of vision. Graham, with his insider knowledge, told us that the glass in the windows is tinted and designed to reflect everything outside, and that higher up, just past the cloud line, there are no windows at all. All we are really seeing is vague and embittering hope.

'Don't look at it,' Troy shakes my hand, surprising me out of my reverie. 'You'll get dizzy again. And you may be small, Rob, but I'll not be able to carry you all the way back!'

I look down at his dark hand that has taken my pale one. His fingers move comfortably into the gaps between mine. I squeeze. We stand in the central reservation and blink at each other for a moment. Argos, who had been sniffing in a bank of laurel off to the side, comes barrelling out with a whimper. She obviously disturbed something's nest.

Troy lets go of my hand gently.

*

At the base of the Tower, there is a series of vast steel stilts on which it sits. Legs, Martha calls them. Each one is as wide as a block of flats and who knows how tall. Graham says they're built so deep underground that the Tower will never fall. Rooted.

Troy and I head to the Leg nearest to us. It has metal rungs attached to the outside. They lead all the way up to the first floor, but it is hard to look that far up on a sunny day. It isn't easy to cope with this dizzying height with a heavy load, but there is one of those metal tubes around it to protect us from falling. Or, at least, to give us the idea that we're protected. Troy goes first and I follow, kissing Argos on the head before I do. She'll wait – she always does. Small brown paws laid out before her, splashed-white nose to the ground.

For forty minutes or so, it is up, up. It is claustrophobic, disconcerting. If you think about the humming grim space, you can't help but cry. So, you focus on the clang of Troy's boots on the rungs, the huff and sighs of his physical exertions. You relish the occasional drop of his sweat falling onto you, because it reminds you that he is living and that he is just above you and that he sees you as Robin and that back there in the lovely open air, he held your hand.

My hair, growing all too long again, sticks to the back of my neck. It is too warm in the metal tunnel, too dark. It is best not to think of what might happen to us, should we get caught.

Or what might await us at the top.

Or what they might throw down the tube in some medieval attempt to ward us off.

It is best to remind yourself of all the things you don't know. Imagine, for example, the people who use our services. Best to remember that our services are called for. We serve a purpose. To remember, Robin, that we are not the enemy. Just humble servants.

*

The hardest part is when we reach the top. We have to heave ourselves over the parapet onto a damp concrete platform that, even in the height of summer, winds you with its chill. The unloading bay. A place of important business, but the unassuming door into the Tower wouldn't look out of place in an office block. We know better than to try to open it. Aleks almost went deaf from the alarms that he set off, that awful day he tried. We found him at the base of the Tower, one ear bleeding. Martha screaming up the ladder to us to hurry. So loudly, so obviously, so attention-seekingly that we were sure she thought him dead.

Troy helps to heave me over the top. We both sit against a slick wall, breathing heavily. Troy takes out his bottle of water and we slurp some down. It tastes of purifier and salt from his lips. I think of Aleks and Martha, cuddled at breakfast. I shake my head.

'Do you ever wonder what it would be like to live here?' Troy asks, nodding to the door and tucking his bottle away.

'Used to,' I admit, looking down at my hands. Almost two years in the wild has hardened them up. They feel like they belong to me now. They are not the hands of that friend, that girl from before. 'But only 'cos I was weighing my options.'

Troy nods. He gets it. We all chose this. Better to be out than in. Better to be true than hidden away. Better to have your feet on the ground. Yes, it is cold and dark in the winter. Yes, I miss warm showers, but not as much as I would miss Argos, or muddy earth beneath my shoes, or the northern, summer night skies that never quite fade to black. Stars everywhere, brighter than the weak glow from the central strip of Tower windows.

I've heard that in parts of Europe, they've sought refuge underground, in bunkers of some sort. I don't know if that is true – Martha doesn't allow us to keep track of the news. It is all lies, anyway. Lies spread by the troops of thugs down here that they call the Hand on the Land.

Not that they come near us. I think they prefer to ignore our existence.

We don't bother anyone, and so no one bothers us.

It is the closest thing to freedom we may ever know.

I readjust into a crouching position. Troy follows suit, understanding the need to be ready to move. We wait in companionable silence.

'I like it,' Troy smiles, his teeth white in the grey light. 'Our life.'

I feel my face redden. 'Whose?'

Troy shrugs. 'Our life,' he points towards me. 'All of us, together.'

'Together?' Unwittingly, it comes out as a question, rather than a statement. Troy inhales, a small grin on his face.

'We've got time to work it all out, right?'

I nod, rendered quiet by the promise in his words. And yet, do we have time? I don't know. After all, we might be living in our grave, the Tower a huge tombstone, a monument to what has passed before. Soon, we might be the brought-to-life version of those propaganda cartoons they posted through the letter boxes a few years ago, when it all went down. We could be the true image of those cartoonish wizened victims. Sure, we may have survived for two years, but what about five? Every day, do we ingest plants grown in poisoned soil? And what about the rains and the floods? They devastated the bottom part of the allotment – now our home – once before. What is to say they won't do that again?

The door opens and scares my ruminations away. A figure dressed in blue stands there. Size and stature would suggest it is a woman, but who am I to judge? We hop to our feet, wave sheepishly. She(?) shoves out a large wooden crate with her foot and backs away as we move towards it. It is stamped with the symbol of the crown. An ironic use of government storage, to hold loot. The woman is wearing a face mask. We wonder, as we always do at this point, what she knows about the world we live in that we don't.

Troy and I unpack the bounty from our backpacks into the crate, our hands brushing as we do. We shove it all back over to the door. She pulls the crate in with gloved hands.

'Thank you,' she says, her voice muffled. Then places a bundle at the threshold and shuts the door.

The bundle contains several letters, folded neatly in envelopes with *to whomever it may concern, thank you,* scrawled in different variations of the shaky handwriting of one who has almost forgotten how to write. At the bottom, there is a list the length of Aleks's ponytail.

'This should keep us busy,' I say, as I tuck it into my backpack.

'Graham will not be pleased,' Troy laughs. We walk towards the hole in the floor that leads back out into the wonderful green world.

'Ready?' Troy asks. 'You want to go first this time?'

I shake my head. 'You go.'

'I'll be waiting for you, at the bottom,' he says, his brown eyes shining.

*

We read the letters on the way home. Our bags empty, sharing out Troy's refreshments (KitKats and a sharing bag of ready salted crisps, only two months out of date and still crunchy), a bottle of real Coke passing between us. What a treat. We normally keep the own-brand stuff for ourselves, it is less popular up in the Tower.

There is the usual outpouring of gratitude for us for helping. The description of what they'll do with the contraband we supply, what they're going to barter for, proving that they're good people really, even if they are using the black market. Then come the lists, the information, the addresses:

'…please, can you go to number 84 (fourth floor, but the lift never worked) and see if my cat is still there? He's called Archie and he…'

'…if it isn't impossible, can you visit my nan's house (13 Acorn Road) and see if there is still this photo of her on her wedding day? There aren't weddings up here and I remember her dress was so…'

'…we used to live in the house on the end of the street, with the big blue door? In the cellar, there is a chest full of baby clothes that I would love to ha…'

'Do you notice how no one asks for us to find their money? Or their jewellery?' Troy sighs, looking up from the cat letter with wet eyes. I catch a glimpse of a past, younger Troy, slung artfully across a sofa, a tabby on his lap. I wonder who else he shared this imaginary home with. I wonder where they are now?

'What would you ask for?' I watch Argos as she weaves in and out of the shadows on the tarmac. Shadows that are starting to lengthen once again, 'if you were up there?' I nod to the building behind us, with its empty, faceless windows.

Troy laughs. 'To be down here, duh!'

*

When we get back to camp, they've transformed it. Aleks is stringing up the last of the bunting that I found a while back in someone's shed. It trails from each of our cabins in turn and back to mine. A pentagon of bright flags, us safely within it. Graham has a fresh vat of his homebrew prepped, a ladle sticking out the top, a hopeful glint of silver in the late afternoon sunlight. Martha has found some candles and is decorating the food table with them. I pull the warehouse whisky from my bag and receive a round of applause, a cheer.

As the sun goes back behind the Tower, we toast its reign. In the light of the fire, everyone's cheeks beat with their life-blood, hot beneath the surface. I scoop Argos into my arms.

'To being down here,' I say to the group.

'To being down here!' they agree and smile at Argos as she nuzzles my neck. Troy holds his cup out to me. We nod at each other, and drink.

Juliet's Fate

Elena wasn't sentimental, nor was she family-driven. She was career minded, always had been. She didn't love the surprise in someone's face when she told them that no, she wasn't married and no, she didn't have children, nor had she wanted them and yes, yes, she was quite slight and spry for someone her age, but she did love her dog.

Elena wasn't stubborn, but she refused to go anywhere the terrier couldn't. They had been together Before, and when they learnt that the Towers didn't admit dogs, here they were in the After: each other's only company.

Best friends, they slowed down together. Got wheezier. All of their six legs seemed to cause them pain.

And then, one day, Juliet left. And now, for Elena, any other task was nigh impossible. The first grey morning without the terrier's company, she applied herself diligently to fastening the tarps tighter around the windows of the derelict park-warden's cottage they called 'home' and seeking out more firewood from one of the fallen trees nearby and purifying the abundant rainwater she had collected in the least rusty bin she could find.

She did every job with a dog whistle clamped in her jaw. With every exhale, she silently begged Juliet to come 'home', back to the park, so that they could take their evening walk and see what they could scrounge.

By lunchtime – a scant meal of lukewarm chickpeas straight from one of the tins she'd found in the empty, half-flooded flats down by the ever-swollen river – she decided enough was enough. She fished out her rucksack from the red tarp she called 'the wardrobe' and filled it with a couple more tins (kidney beans, and glory of all glories a tin of actual Heinz baked beans), her lightest water bottle (a squishable milk carton), a couple of smaller tarps and Juliet's blanket. Before folding it up, she held it to her nose for a moment and inhaled not only the dog's bacon and egg smell, but also many little hairs. Elena spent the first few minutes of her journey with her hand clamped over her nose, trying to sneeze as quietly as possible. As she walked, she dragged her dark eyes across her surroundings. She was developing a headache.

Elena didn't think of herself as a creature of habit, but her route towards town just happened to be their usual evening walk. The humid weather had turned it into a paradise for the opportune. She checked her socks were high up her leggings as the long grass brushed against them. Part of their pre-sleep routine was a tick check. Juliet would turn onto her back in anticipation, despite the rush of the wind at the door or the cry of some unknown beast. Elena didn't hold her joy against her, she hadn't yet forgotten how comforting it was to be touched by a kind, trusted hand, even if it had to twist a horrible little creature out of your skin.

Brambles grabbed at Elena as she took what was once the main path. She scanned and scanned, already exhausted by the brightness of the day. The glow of the sunless white sky was relentless, it hummed at her with urgency. The Tower, just to the right of her vision, tore the sky. She put her whistle to her downturned mouth and silently screamed across the overgrown mess.

There was no wind, but here and there patches of grass shook. Branches danced about. Every so often, Elena tricked herself into seeing a flash of a tail as white as cow parsley, of hearing a bark that sounded almost exactly like the crack of a twig under foot. Thinking about the sort of person who might live in this section of the park, near the leg of the Tower, forced Elena to pick up the pace. She blew panicked short blasts. *Mayday!* she whistled, thinking about the smallness of Juliet's paw on the backpack the two shared as a pillow, *come back to me now, there's a good girl!*

By the time she reached the river, she was out of breath. The closer she got to town, the thicker the air became. Up the hill, the air had been almost fresh. Now, it tasted sour with ash and something unnameable, but so sweet it caught in her throat. She coughed so hard she tasted blood. She swallowed quickly. She didn't dare check the phlegm. Elena wasn't naïve, but not noticing problems was as good as not having them.

The bridge she was supposed to cross had fallen victim to a fire. There was one charred plank to cross. She put her hands on her knees and bent over for a moment, her breath still short in her lungs. She looked behind her, blowing hard on the whistle, hoping Juliet would give the game up and flash into view, relieving her of the duty she was now bound to fulfil. Elena hadn't been out alone since everything changed. As she stared back towards 'home', the undergrowth began to rise up where she had trampled it down. Within seconds, she had no idea which path she had taken. Elena wasn't scared, not as such.

She was forced to go on.

*

There was more evidence of human life the nearer she got to the centre of town – the glow of fires in above-shop windows and the echo of footsteps on the high street. There were definitely some of them living in the huge Primark, because she could see piles of boxes in one of the second-floor display windows, blocking out the glare. If Juliet had been trotting beside her, Elena would have whispered some joke that they hadn't been left behind at all, that the high street had just been taken back to the 1980s. It didn't meet with the same ear-cocked interest when she told it to herself, but her cracked lips felt the pain of a smile.

Now that she was used to the idea of a journey, Elena had a destination in mind. Like all mad dogs, Juliet loved the beach. Elena had no choice but to start her search there. It would take a day and a half, because Elena was creaky and thinner than ever. Only a few years ago, Elena ran this very same route with about 30,000 other people. Continuously scanning the environment, Elena walked the centre of the road, imagining cheering supporters on the pavements. She could almost feel the sun on her back, the swish of her long grey ponytail threatening to stick in her armpits. On the high street, there was an empty checkpoint. No guards to be seen and as Elena sniffed around the small cabin, no sign of recent life. It felt like The Hand had all but deserted the city centre. Elena hoped this was the case.

As she reached the Art Deco cinema, she had to stop for breath. Had she been running? It was hard to tell, with no squat and slow Juliet beside her to set the pace. She gasped in the thick air and pushed her hair off her face, slicked it down with the drizzle. It was in that annoying stage of growing-back-ness that meant it was always in her eyes. She looked at herself in the window of a café opposite.

There were two people in the reflection.

She had stopped scanning.

The stranger stood on the opposite side of the road and stared. She leant her head against the window, sucking in more mouthfuls of the foul air. She screwed her eyes tight shut. She blew on the whistle, three short rasps.

Elena wasn't good with surprises. She tried to calm herself. She thought of the beach and of Juliet and counted as high as she could remember to. When she turned, and forced her eyes open, the person was still there, their head cocked to one side as if listening to her. Elena sniffed the air, but the person was too far away to get a good enough sense of their character.

'Y'alright there?'

Elena obviously didn't seem threatening to the figure, who stood with their legs slightly apart and their arms across their chest. Their heavy work boots ended near their knees. Elena was warm with envy at their sturdy looking sides and heavy soles. They looked too well-made to have been commissioned by The Hand. In her coat pocket, her hand sought the penknife that she had tucked away the day the river flooded and she'd had to move uphill.

She ran her thumb along its silver side and tried to calm herself.

'I like your boots.' She swallowed down some bitter tasting saliva. Elena wasn't the best at conversation, but she knew enough. Compliments always calmed you down. Her voice came out in a rasp: 'A-and I've lost my dog, Juliet. Have you seen her? She's a terrier, with a br–'

The figure shook their head slowly and then shrugged. 'I hope she wasn't chunky.' The laugh was a bark, deep from the stomach. Unnatural, underused.

'She… we don't have much to eat,' Elena held her empty hands up to the leaden sky, 'so how could she be chunky?'

The figure shrugged again, shook one leg out and then the other. 'Not likely to be eaten then, is she, this Juliet?'

Elena thought better of releasing the howl in her chest. She shook her head dumbly.

'Right then,' the figure started to turn away. 'Good luck with your search.'

Elena wasn't able to speak. She forced herself off the window, gave herself a shake. She placed her feet more firmly on the cracked pavement. Beneath her peeling trainers, the red graffiti read: *It is never too late!*

'Oi!' The figure hollered and Elena looked up again with a whimper. The figure was closer than before, on her side of the road, three or four metres from her. She could smell them now – unwashed flesh and metal filings. She let out a soft growl, backed herself further against the cinema's entrance.

'My boots,' the figure yawned, and acid filled Elena's nose. 'They're from a place in South Shields. One of the last things I bought in an actual shop!'

Elena forced out a 'Thank you.'

The figure shrugged for the third time and began to walk away from her, their hands jammed deep into the pockets of their long raincoat. Elena thought better of telling them how much she admired the coat too. Elena wasn't foolish.

What with the sudden shock of the person's presence, the chickpeas were also working their magic. Somewhere, Juliet must be doing her stuff, Elena hoped, because the two of them were like clockwork. Elena still found it funny, when they would squat down opposite each other in a place Juliet deemed suitable. Since today was so strange already, Elena decided to head into the cinema and try her luck with an actual toilet. Or that is what she told herself. Really, she just wanted to lock herself somewhere for a moment and bring Juliet's blanket to her face.

Juliet hadn't always been around, but, Elena admitted to herself, as she pushed open the glass doors at the cinema's darkened entrance, Juliet had marked a new beginning. Before Juliet, Elena had always been a selfish person. Self-sufficient, she called it, driven. An offence to a relationship, her last partner had called it, before exiting her life as brilliantly and attractively as he had arrived. The loss of love: of cups of tea and evening de-briefs and Sunday trips to the beach, prompted Elena to head to the rescue centre on the Great North Road. She'd always known it was there. On Sunday strolls, the bright sign always caught her eye. Long before she'd arrived, Juliet had been housed there, sharing a kennel with another Jack Russell. They had been found together in an empty bin at the edge of the moor. Their puppy legs had been too short to climb out. Elena's finding Juliet, and Juliet's finding Elena, hadn't wiped either of their pasts clean. Elena longed for Juliet to speak to her like a human. Juliet never went near rubbish bins. And yet, Juliet's face at the window when Elena got home, the light picking up its unruly edge of fuzz, definitely acted as a shock absorber.

Elena wasn't a natural crier, but tears grew hot in her eyes. She stood in the dark foyer of the cinema and blinked in surprise. She put the dog whistle to her lips and blew as hard as she could, her dirty cheeks puffing so far out, she could just about see them if she looked down.

Elena decided against looking for a light switch. She didn't know who could be living in the cinema. The ticket desks had been ransacked for anything useful – there were no pens, no reams of paper left. Both keyboards were gone and of course, the office chairs would have been looted as soon as everything had started to dissolve. Anything that had wheels. Beside her was a set of stairs and she could just make out the sign for the toilets. She started to climb.

'I wouldn't.' A small voice, from somewhere near the ticket desk.

'W-wouldn't what?' Elena cleared her throat, narrowing her eyes in the dark. She sniffed, licked the air. She could sense no threat. Elena wasn't scared. She took a step back down towards the foyer.

'Go up there.' The small voice again. 'I wouldn't go up there.'

Elena, out of habit more than anything now, let out a long blow on the whistle. Then she tucked it into her coat pocket. I'm here, Juliet. Come find me.

'I just wanted to use the toilet.'

'That's for paying customers only.' The person howled with laughter. The bare bulb in the centre of the foyer shuddered with the sudden volume.

'I – I have nothing to give,' Elena admitted, hoping whoever was there wouldn't check her bag and find the blankets and tins. They'd have every right. She was trespassing. 'I'll go now.'

'Nah, don't.' The voice belonged to a smallish girl, maybe about ten, who stepped out from behind one of the central pillars. 'Mam'll kill me if you don't at least pop in.'

'That's kind.' Elena was put off by how small the girl seemed in the dying light and how old she sounded. 'But I need to get a step on... I've got to be somewhere.'

'It's almost dark.' The girl's voice dropped lower. 'Come on.'

Elena turned to look out of the glass doors and it was true, the sun – or whatever it was that kept the light on nowadays – had disappeared. *Goodnight sun,* Elena said to herself, *goodnight Juliet.* Elena wasn't ready to give up, but the likelihood of seeing either of them again shrank a little in her mind.

Elena's bowels twisted as a clammy hand insisted on holding hers.

'I said, come on!' The hand pulled her towards another set of steps that led to the basement cinema. Elena looked behind her, but the gloom seemed to offer a spectacle of shapes that could have been any of her worst nightmares. She didn't see Juliet either, and that was so much worse. She raised her empty hand in surrender and moved forward.

The hand pulled hard, almost toppling Elena at the top of the stairs. 'There are toilets down here too,' the girl explained, 'and you can always pretend that there is running water.'

'Pretend?' Elena croaked, her stomach still in dismay, desperate now.

'Yes, it is what we do here.'

'Well, I guess it was a cinema…'

The small hand squeezed hers and then let it go. They stood just inside the cinema doors. The smell of bodies in the semi dark was overpowering. Elena bent double and vomited a few sharp-tasting chickpeas into the corner. It did not smell like she was the first one to have done this. She put her hand out for her little guide, but she had disappeared. Elena wasn't offended, not after making such a spectacle of herself.

The huge space that once held the screen was directly in front of her. Beneath it, a small fire glowed. An image of an actor whose name was just on the tip of her tongue was burnt onto the screen, like it had been left up there too long. As Elena's eyes grew accustomed to the dark, she could make out the rows of cinema seats and the presence of quite a few heads. It was like an off-peak midday viewing of a not-very-popular film.

'Do you know who that actor up there is?' A hand waved close to Elena's face.

'N-no,' Elena admitted. She wasn't a film buff. She was exhausted. She had gone from talking only to a dog for months on end, to talking to three people in one hour. 'But it'll come to me.'

'I've been here since the rains, and it still hasn't come to me.' The voice belonged to a woman – Elena could tell by the lack of fear in its timbre. 'You've met wor Lisa, I see?'

'Your daughter?'

'Aye, that's the one.'

'Yeah, she said I had to come down.'

'Is it dark?'

'Almost.'

'She wasn't wrong. You get some strange things happening in town at night. It's not like being tucked away somewhere safe up the hill.'

'Nothing has changed then?' Elena put a smile on, to make it clear her barbed comment was a joke. The cinema was full of whispers and muted discussions. It made sense to Elena. It was peaceful.

'You don't have to talk to any of us. But you can sleep here.'

'It isn't that I don't want to talk.' Elena wasn't willing to be rude.

'It's just that you don't know what to say?' The woman's voice was light with a grin. 'I could find you a script?'

'A script?'

'Oh yeah, we put on plays every night. From whoever we've got staying. Tonight, it is *Romeo and Juliet*, but we're yet to find our female lead.'

I know the feeling. Elena sighed, peeling her sticky coat off her back. She placed it on the nearest cinema seat. Someone had hacked away at the row behind her, removing all of the arms so that a person could lie down properly. Elena hoped one day to meet this vandal and thank them for their gift to society. She bunched her backpack up with her coat like a pillow. Her shoulders raised in anticipation.

'What brings you here?'

Elena explained to the woman standing at her shoulder about her quest.

'Is that why you didn't leave when we were told?'

'Yeah, they wouldn't accept dogs, so we stayed behind.' And then, with effort, 'Why are you still here?'

'My daughter is blind.' Elena felt the woman's shoulders rise and fall in a shrug. 'They wouldn't have taken her.'

Elena searched the air in front of her desperately, hoping that an adequate sentence would form itself. Elena wasn't eloquent.

'C-can I use the toilets?'

The woman said she could, with a smile back on her face. Elena thanked her. As she moved away, the floor rumbled beneath her feet.

'Do the trains run still?' Elena asked her new host, her mind wreaking havoc with her as image after image of a Metro-maimed Juliet tore through her. The woman said nothing, so Elena tried again:

'Sorry – did you feel the train?'

The woman said nothing for a moment or two and then responded, further away and in a cautious voice, 'I did not.'

*

Elena was taking a good long time in the toilets, and this allowed the group – who called themselves the Theatre Group at the End of the World – to find their Juliet. A woman about a decade younger than Elena, with a clear whisper and good enough eyesight to read in the almost dark. She had stumbled in, much like Elena, looking for somewhere to rest. In her sequestered seats, Elena listened to their terse whispers with relief. They seemed very intent on doing a good job, despite the odds stacked against them by the lack of light, staging and, Elena surmised, much talent. Elena wasn't sentimental, but she traced the plaque on the back of the seat in front of her with a gnarled, dry finger.

For mam, who always bought popcorn. And for dad, who always let me share it.

The sponge of the battered seats and the hushed voices of the raconteurs reminded Elena of falling asleep in a softly lit bedroom, the sound of a radio elsewhere in the house, the noises of existence in some adjacent room, the feeling of her head pouring onto the soft, freshly washed pillow and the middle of her body, attached to some sort of gravitational lasso…

'I saw your dog.'

By the feel of breath on Elena's face, the girl was standing right above her makeshift bed. Elena yelped and a cacophony of 'sssssshhhh' filled the velvety room. She scrambled to sit up, her hand clutched tight around the dog whistle.

'You saw Juliet?' Elena frowned. 'But how?'

'Rude.'

'No, I didn't mean it like that. Sorry. Where did you see her?'

Silence.

'Lisa?'

Nothing.

Elena put out her hand, and swiped the air all around her. She hissed the child's name into the dark. Someone in the next row told her to shut up. Elena blew the whistle until her lips hummed with the pain of it.

Her beloved plush bed now seemed the equivalent of a rock. Elena curled up as foetally as she could. Her nose stung with the salt as she blinked away at the thoughts of the absent wiry bottom that had for the past fifteen years, if not longer, wiggled itself to sleep against her hip.

*

The shelves of the chemist were empty and covered in shards of glass. Here and there a battery-powered light still flickered in a cabinet, but the fridges had long since lost their power. Elena scoured the normal sections before crawling on hands and knees to look under the pharmacy cabinets, in hope of–

'Yes, Juliet! Look what I found!'

Silence. Elena's hand shook a little as she held out the small pot of shop-brand moisturiser, its plastic container slightly melted, but the foil covering seemingly intact. She ripped it open and decorated her fingertips with cooling globs of relief. She covered her blotched face. Moisturiser stung its way into the cracks, paying heed to her skin's cry for more, putting out the fires of injustice that still raged in Elena after last night's cinema trip. A low growl at it all and Elena was on her feet again.

She ran her hand along the bottom of the food cabinet, she stuck her fingers into gaps in shelves. She secured a tired and bent Curly Wurly and a bottle of full fat Coke. She blew the whistle in victory and left.

It was still early, the glare not yet too high to make scanning the horizon a headache. She reached the Tyne Bridge quicker than she'd expected. Once again, the checkpoint was empty. Below her, the river gushed apace. The cafes and bars on the quayside were all but submerged. Lampposts stuck out above the murky brown. Her teeth (still all hers, Elena wasn't yet ready for dentures) clamped to each other with the ache of caramel, she walked the centre of the dual carriageway. She was alone, save for the vapours of long since passed cars. Signs posted every five metres or so told her that she was not alone, that the best was yet to come, that somebody loved her. The number offering her solace would no longer be in service, surely? Juliet, her good Samaritan, however, would soon be back by her side.

The greyish light blinked through each spoke of the iron structure as she passed along. As she reached the centre of the bridge, the swollen river disappeared from beneath her feet. Fog enveloped it. She hummed, taking in the smashed glass panes of the Sage and the graffiti-covered face of the Baltic. On one corner, something seemed to be hanging from a rope, a dead-weight in the windless morning. Elena looked the other way. She watched the green of an army truck speeding across the swing bridge to her right. She thought of Juliet with a tyre mark across her side. She sped up, twisting the whistle between fingers still slick with moisturiser.

Once across the river, she allowed herself a swig of Coke. The bubbles caught in between her teeth and she was, for one moment, nothing but sweet pain. And then the joy of it all kicked in.

The hill to undo her descent into town awaited her.

Of course, she vomited it all up. Her body rejected the pop in bouts of oily anger. Up came the chocolate bar, a twisted mass of sugar, knotted in her stomach. Her retching echoed along the empty dual carriageway as she passed Gateshead Stadium. Elena, a woman who had always tried to do the right thing, wasn't embarrassed, she was too tired.

Juliet would have cleared the mess up for her and it would have killed the little dog. Elena was glad that she was protected in her absence, but her hand at her side clutched the whistle.

The further from town, the more empty cars she saw. Had they been abandoned on a family trip to the coast? What had caused their drivers to stop and flee? Every window she walked past was smashed and all the seats were empty, but occasionally there was a blink of a headlamp, causing Elena – in shock, or in fear – to bend double again. She was leaving Juliet breadcrumbs in neat little piles of sick. In her right cheek, her tongue worried at an oncoming blister. Salt water would fix it all. Salt water and Juliet.

*

When she reached the avenue, it was the afternoon. The shops along the high-street had long been ransacked. Everything was broken glass and scorch marks and red writing. Symbols she didn't recognise, religious scriptures she did. Elena wasn't religious, but she had been brought up going to church. She had first tried to seek safety in a church, when the end came and people fled to the Towers, but all the doors she'd tried were locked, and she wasn't one to go where she wasn't wanted.

Still, she blew her whistle in prayer. Elena was unwilling to give in to the sensation of the world – this new one, the one as she knew it – being off-kilter. She took gulps of the air, now beginning to freshen and become salty, as she urged herself to keep going.

Across the road from her, a shop caught her eye. Upon closer inspection, it was a shoe shop. She thought back to the stranger she had met in town, only yesterday. The one who had introduced to her the idea the Juliet was fair game, now that she was out and about in the world.

Elena stepped through the doorway (the door had long ago been torn from its hinges) and stood in front of what must have been, at one point, the cashier's desk.

'I'd like those boots,' she tells the empty room, and feels her hairs stand on end at the sound of her own voice. 'The tall, warm-looking ones.'

Elena wasn't sure what she had been expecting. After a moment, she moved behind the front desk and into the stock room, which had once been separated by a curtain made from many strips of plastic. Something had happened to it and it was now a sticky clumped mass of brown and yellow.

The stock room smelt of recently smoked cigarettes. Elena wasn't going to stay long. Taking advantage of the shelter and the privacy, she squatted down in an empty corner, by some shelves and relieved herself. She blew the whistle as she did. *I've been here, my girl.*

As she hunkered down, Elena almost over-balanced, and her arm shot out to the shelves to support her. As she pulled her arm away, her jacket caught on the corner of one shelf and dislodged the entire structure.

Elena, arms over her head, cowered against the rain of cardboard boxes and the cacophony of metal on hard, concrete floor. Her ears rang with the noise.

Not only Juliet would know where she was, now.

She hurried to pull her trousers up, to pick her way out of the room, which was now a pile of half-open shoe boxes.

Half open.

The boots.

89

She could see them – the same tough leather, the fluffy looking trim.

She held her breath, kicked the box on its side.

Her size.

She felt hot liquid on her cheeks, she blew her whistle in glee.

She picked the box up in shaking hands, carried it back out into the main shop. She sat on what was left of a stool. Mice – or worse – had obviously been at the filling. She pulled the boots out of the box and as she did so, a coin fell to the floor.

With a grunt, she bent down to pick it up.

It was a silver medallion that read:

If found, please call Elena Dossantos.

07734 121 8397

It was the tag to Juliet's collar.

*

Elena wasn't a thief, but the boots were on a level of comfort she'd forgotten existed. She left her tired old trainers in the store, with a rushed promise scribbled on a note assuring the long-lost owners that she would pay for the boots, eventually.

Despite her joyful feet, the beach couldn't come soon enough. Juliet would be waiting for her.

She blew her whistle: *I'm coming, I'm coming.*

The approach to the shoreline was downhill and although her breath was now short and sharp, she couldn't help but speed up. She knew she could hear Juliet yapping at the waves.

Juliet would be waiting for her.

Then, quicker than predicted, there was the sea. And just before it, a sliver of sand.

Pale and yellow and empty.

No small body, no paw prints.

Seaweed and bracken had been neatly organised by the sea into little piles. The sound of the water played with Elena's ears. She wobbled until eventually, she sat down hard on her bum in the cold sand, her new boots almost in the water.

*

'Nice boots.'

Elena sat, the cold from the sand creeping into her buttocks. She turned to look and saw a new officer, kinder seeming than the one she had been speaking to earlier. They were part of the local law enforcement, led by the Hand, but nowhere near as threatening as she had supposed. She accepted the blanket he held out to her and wrapped it around her bony shoulders.

'Have you seen Juliet?' she asked him.

It had just gone six in the morning. The first officer, the one who had found Elena and introduced himself as Steve, sighed tiredly. He beckoned to his newcomer colleague and the two men stepped a few metres away from her. Elena was not hard of hearing. According to their conversation, Steve had had quite a night of it:

'I'm telling you, Ben,' he complained to the new official, 'I spent three hours with this one proper mental lass with this huge black dog, both of them ranting and raving, asking if I'd seen her brother who was meant to be coming back off the rigs any day now. Soon as that had been dealt with (sent her back where she came from, told her to wait for him there) this one turns up. Says her name is Elena. She's looking for her dog – Juliet – and all. What a name! Tell me Ben, what is it with people and pets? Can't they see the apocalypse is coming? That it is only getting worse? Back when we had television, I watched a programme about that nuclear crisis that happened in Russia, you know the one with all the fire–'

'Chernobyl?'

'Aye, that's it – when Chernobyl happened, they just shot all the house pets when people evacuated the cities. I'd sign up to that. Shoot them all.'

'Best not write all of that in your report, Steve,' Ben told him, causing Elena to laugh, once, like a bark. The two men glanced at her, then Ben continued: 'The boss is a cat person. And anyway, don't your daughters have a hamster?'

'Aye they do! I'll tell you, you've got another think coming if you think I'm going to take that rodent with me when it comes time for us to head up to the Towers!'

Ben, seemingly unable to help himself, laughed out hot steams of breath.

Elena looked out across the water as the men talked. Overnight, the temperature must have dropped, and it must have been quite choppy. In the beginning light, she could see that some boats had caught on the rocks around the tiny Herd Groyne lighthouse.

'Look at them all,' Steve continued, gesturing to the sea. 'We told them NOT to get in the boats, of course. And then when they did get in, we told them NOT to get in too close to the lighthouse. And when they did get in too close to the lighthouse, the North Sea showed them what's what. Now what are we supposed to do?'

Elena looked at the lighthouse, a 'beacon' of hope for long-dead sailors. Tens of boats were stuck, wrecked against its walls, unable to get back off.

'There was some screaming,' Steve informed Ben as he tucked into the sausage roll his colleague had brought him. Both men looked over at Elena guiltily, but she refused to engage with them. She kept her watering eyes on the boats. 'But I couldn't for the life of me work out if it was from over there,' Steve gestured to the lighthouse. The three people watched those who were stranded wave pieces of material at them for a moment. 'Or over here,' Steve threw out his hand, motioning ahead of them. 'Then I met her.' He pointed to Elena again. She sat there, small and cold.

Ben coughed, resignedly. 'There are definitely more boats now, aren't there?'

Elena found herself nodding. Every sort of vessel that vaguely resembled a boat, some water-tight and some not so much, stretched ahead of them. A desperate patchwork of clinking metal and the dull thuds of wood on wood. They steadied each other as they rocked on the water. There was no real space for movement. They ranged from the lighthouse and looped further around the coast, heading towards Tynemouth. There were a good few still dotted on the shore, waiting to push off. Their occupants seemed to be dozing in the gentle rocking, the carpet of boats was quiet. Further out, Elena watched a figure walk across three or four boats before finally finding what they were looking for and dropping down into the tarpaulin-covered safety of the hull. Pretty nimble. She glanced over at the rotund men. Could they keep that sort of balance? Or would they fall? Into what, though? Not in the sea, that's for sure.

There was not a big enough gap anywhere.

'They're reaching the windmills,' Steve commented, through pastry-covered lips. Elena wished he'd hurry up and go away. She was bored of his voice.

Ben and Elena followed the direction of Steve's hi-viz hand. The wind turbines had been planted about fifteen years previously – optimistically, foolishly, the government's last-ditch attempt to woo the north-east with unfounded promises – a good few miles out to sea. They played tricks with Elena's eyes, disappearing into the sea with the curve of the planet.

Steve was right. Some boats had obviously set off already. Dots of humanity motored through the dawn, past their mechanical stems and off out towards some sort of far north salvation.

'Hey, why do Norwegian sailors wear black and white uniforms?' Steve asked, finishing up his breakfast with a belch.

'I don't know Steve,' Ben sighed. 'Why do Norwegian sailors wear–'

'So that they can Scandinavian when they return to port,' Elena said quietly. Steve frowned at her, but laughed uncertainly. She rolled her eyes. 'Scan-the-navy-in,' she repeated, and when Ben still didn't smile, she growled slightly. 'Black and white. Like barcodes.'

Steve chuckled at her and at Ben. 'Exactly that, Elena. Nice one.'

Then, with a wave, he headed back towards the green army truck that Ben must have arrived in. A tank full of petrol, source unknown to someone as insignificant as Elena.

'See you this evening, Benny-boy!' Steve shouted, before clambering in.

When he'd driven off, Ben sat down beside Elena. His body was round, and it gave off a welcome warmth. She tried to remain strong, sturdy. She told herself she was commanding the sea. She played with the small metal whistle, passing it between ropey, almost-blue hands.

Then she saw the soil, caked beneath her fingernails, as if she had been digging in earth.

'When did Juliet go missing?' Ben asked.

'Two days ago.'

'Does she normally run away?'

'No. She is mine. I'm hers.'

The pair said nothing. They watched boats bob sleepily on the water. Steam rose from some as breakfast, in all its many haphazard forms, began to be served.

*

Elena wasn't forgetful – she wasn't losing it – she wasn't crazy – but she felt all those things as she sat on the beach, staring out across the myriad boats.

Perhaps it had taken the sea air, the behaviour of the officers of The Hand, if that is who they even were, to shake loose one particular memory. Or maybe it was the metal medallion that had fallen from a pocket and landed in the box. Maybe that had brought it all back to her. The old and now still, white and brown body. The cold fur. The stiff, short legs.

Earth landing on the top of a closed box.

She looked at the whistle, resisted putting it to her lips.

'We can wait for Juliet a while longer,' Ben reached into his pocket and pulled out a boiled sweet. 'Then we can decide what you want to do next. I can put you in touch with services, get you to a Tower. But we'll wait a bit more first. Sound good?'

Elena held the bright yellow sweet against the roar of the grey sea. She looked at her feet, warmly encased in her new boots. She blinked in the greenish sunrise, the dawn of her third morning on earth without Juliet.

'Sounds good,' she agreed.

Ending

2035

Renaissance

No one person can change the world. Every global change is a group effort.

Take the floods and the waves, for example. We caused them. We all drove our cars, we all went on holiday to far-away places on long-haul flights. We all put the plastic container in the normal bin on a Tuesday night when we couldn't be bothered to empty the too-full recycling bin.

There are times when we do something we know is wrong – for example, not recycling – and hope that no one else is doing it.

Spoiler: everyone else is doing it.

I believe, though – and still, after all this – that most of the time, we're not trying to make everything worse.

Most of the time.

*

The shower lessens and then stops cold. My two minutes is up.

It was nice while it lasted. The warm water gave me a moment to think good things about humankind, which doesn't often happen day to day.

To bed, I guess.

The latest book that I've got my hands on – contraband delivered it just last week – is one of my favourites. Clément and I used to read it in competition. I was always racing my teenage son to see who could finish it faster. It made him happy to win – not only because he, a bored teenager with an endless summer ahead of him, was faster than his mum, whose job always kept her busy – but also because he could tell me all the spoilers. Which he relished doing, all of the time.

I can't remember what happens in this one. The journey to the here and now has moved things around, mentally, and I can't quite find the same order in which everything used to sit.

I know I've read the whole series – aside from the last one. I think that I was already sequestered away by the time the author, the esteemed Colleen Nkosi, released it. I'm sure it will come through in that magic crate eventually.

Goodbye to Gaia still feels like escapism, like fiction.

I plump my one pillow as best I can and prop myself up. Open the book. The spine creaks and wafts the smell of mildew straight into my nose. It is bearable, though. It smells like outside. I want to know where it has been. Perhaps I will find hints in its pages. A crushed leaf, a smudge of mud? I remove the dust cover, because I can't bear reading with them. They get caught on the coverlet and rip. I like to keep them pristine.

As I slide it open, a tight, familiar scribble catches my eye. The pencil is faint in the dim light of my quarters, but it still manages to change my world. This one piece of paper.

I knew you'd find this eventually. It is safe down here now. No more rain. No more waves. I'll be waiting for you, at the southern leg. Océane, run free! – Clém.

I am still staring at it when they turn the lights out. How old is it? When did he write it? The latest contraband delivery was two nights ago – but could this mean he sent it then? Or has this book been sitting somewhere, gathering mildew, its interior secrets unrevealed for some time?

When it goes dark, I feel bereft all over again. His writing, his nickname. His love. There is a thrum of abandonment that thuds right through me. I do not know if I gasp for his desertion by me, or of me. Neither of them – he nor his father – ever tried to find me.

Until now.

Somehow, I manage to sleep. Throughout the night, the dust cover stays folded in my hand like a prayer.

*

My father was a tall man with eyebrows that met in the middle. Around my eighth birthday, he had a moustache for a bit, but my mother took a razor to his lip while he slept one night. He did not try to grow it again. After that, we both found sleep a little bit harder, knowing what she was capable of.

They met at work. Both were employees at the space centre. Both programmers. Both worked on modelling potential outcomes, gauging potential risks. It was a shame they couldn't see the torment that was their long and loud marriage.

Maybe they did, and believed it was worth the risk.

I spent a lot of my childhood reading in offices, leaning against huge humming computers and tapping my foot to the clack of a typewriter. Waiting, always, for them to have finished work.

It must have all rubbed off on me. Numbers have always made sense.

*

In the night, I develop a paper cut. The note has soaked up a corner of blood, but it is still legible, just about. As I get my uniform on, I tuck it safely away in the zip pocket just above my breast, near my heart.

Breakfast's gruel is tastier with my secret knowledge. In fact, the lack of good coffee – cruelly, that is one taste I remember from before – doesn't even get me down.

When I start my shift, however, it all comes back.

The server 'room' is more like a great hall. It takes up over half of my storey. On the southern side of the Tower, there is a small boxed off area, which is where I work. There is no label on the door. There is nothing about me that marks me out as Head of Communications for the Power. My uniform is the same blue as any other worker in this sector, as if I worked in the kitchens or the greenhouses. And it is fair enough, I suppose, because there must be many more people within this structure who are more qualified for my job.

It is noisy and chilly in here; cool draughts of air are fanned across the vast space. It is the Power's hub and main source of information for this Tower. Heavy, grinding fans maintain the temperature for these vital electronic beings, these things that mean those in charge can communicate with other countries – if they want to listen – and gauge weather occurrences, deliberate on risks. Machines that facilitate the endless video meets between us up here and The Hand down there.

The cold in the room and the not-quite-full stomach always bathes me in fury, but I run my checks, make sure everything is functioning as it should.

It is repetitive lonely work.

I think of my book, of my son.

no more rain

It can't be true, can it? After all, we need some rain to fall. Am I to take it to mean that there isn't any more rain than normal, for this time of year? Or is it a hoax? Is he trying to lure me to my death? And if he is, why?

And the way he signed it off… it couldn't be anyone but Clém, could it?

*

One of the possible reasons for my having adapted so well to this new life, that I was forced – some might say kidnapped – into, is that I had experienced the loss of my home before.

We left the island of my birth when I was twelve. Kourou – a place now almost entirely underwater – had been home to my father and me since birth. My mum, who had met my father when travelling through south America, was originally from the north-east of England. It was a happy childhood, I think. All I really remember is that fruit was always juicier there.

When my dad lost his job to a man from Paris, whose French passport said that he was just as Guianese as mon papa, we moved to Newcastle.

We made it work. I grew up forgetting my name – Océane – was pronounced Osayanne and thinking it was actually Oshayn.

I developed a happy sing-song accent. I married a man with round brown eyes who ended sentences with words like hinny and pet. My son's voice came out unexpected, rooted in the north-east with only the slightest nod to French in the way he burred his 'r's.

The tropics of my childhood were almost entirely forgotten to me.

Until I read my favourite in the *Goodbye to Gaia* series: *Oceans Run Free*.

*

This is exactly the book I found on my bed, when I got back to my quarters after my shift last night. I could smell that someone had been there recently.

And I start to think, can one person change the world?

I read for as long as they allow. When the lights go out, I run my fingers over the page, willing it to communicate with me. That night I dream of the tropics of my youth, I place my hands on humid tree-trunks and I drink in sweet, heavy-with-water air.

*

The following morning, I snatch an extra half hour for reading by forcing myself to rise when I hear the above storey's generators kick in. Normally, I roll over and have another half hour before the alarm on our level. I am almost halfway through the book when it goes off and I have to go for some sustenance.

Being late makes the officials who are, let's face it, always watching, suspicious.

They can't know that I think of the book all morning. Its words become the code I type as I design the latest part of the Power's site and I have to keep going back to correct myself.

A cough brings me out of my reverie:

'They need a message sent out.'

It is a small, stocky colleague of mine, who always stands with his arms behind his back like he is a soldier. Maybe he was, once, but then he isn't down there, as part of the Hand.

I call him P'tit in my head, because it makes his obvious brawn and generally threatening demeanour slightly less so.

His head is freshly shorn and his ears look cold.

'How urgent?'

'As soon as possible.' Then he adds, 'Before lunch.'

Even with the humming and whirring, both our stomachs audibly grumble.

'For who?'

'All storeys.'

'All citizens?'

'All storeys,' he repeats.

He hands me the information, complete with today's password. Access to the entire, in-Tower comms system is but eleven letters away:

renaissance

I say the word to myself and the squat man shushes me once, then again before stepping back out of humming, whirring room.

I read the message, my eyes reluctant to take in anything in that isn't glorious Gaia.

Citizens: this is a reminder that the requesting, use and exchanging of contraband is both dangerous and a punishable offence.

Anyone caught with contraband will have to face the grave consequences of their actions.

My favourite book, the thing that has made the past few days exciting, is illegal. Perhaps the person who delivered it to me – that kind, giving person – has already been caught.

I think of Clém's note, the power of his words. His world-changing note.

I start to type.

*

The communication screen in my room is screaming and honking when I finally get back. I have spent the afternoon edging around corners and stepping into cupboards so as to avoid meeting any colleagues. They were nowhere to be seen. Despite not wanting to be caught, I feel left out. What important meeting is being held that I am missing?

Océane, run free!

They will be able to trace me. I don't have long.

I don't want to take a lot with me. Just the yellow coat they gave me when I arrived, spare socks in one pocket, spare underwear in the other.

Of course, I take the books in my rucksack.

I am reevaluating that decision, thinking about the many stairs I will soon have to descend with their brilliant weight on my back when I am distracted by noises outside my door. Are they coming for me already?

Scuffles, slams, shouts.

The corridor, usually deathly quiet, sounds like an outdoor protest.

No, they are stealthier than that. I've seen them take people away. I've helped track criminals through the very same system I just hacked.

They zone in and tweezer out the culprit in the night.

My aim is to open my door just a crack, to peek at the occurrences, but as I open it, a person falls through into my room. The corridor is full to crushing point. More faces than I have seen in years. Shorn heads, sharp shoulders. I feel a nausea akin to sea sickness, watching them watch me. The person who fell into my quarters looks to have winded himself. He rolls awkwardly on the floor, his backpack making it difficult for him to right himself. His hands clutch at his stomach. I turn to reach out to him, but as I do, the stalled line moves. My own rucksack, full of literary cargo, is sandwiched between two people. I

100

am pulled along, away from my room. I am small and weak in the face of the crowd's desire to move. I have no choice but to move too.

I am carried towards the stairs and then deposited. I stand, adjusting to the sudden lack of movement. People rush past me. They have already begun their long descent.

I have no choice, now.

The stairwell is full of breathless susurrations.

'No more rain!'

'It is safe!'

I am struggling to breathe – not only because of the pack and my already aching thighs – but because the turn of events – and perhaps my role in it – is beginning to catch up with me. There is a woman beside me who seems to be more annoyed then out of breath. She tuts whenever the line stalls. At times, she rolls her eyes.

'Are you alright?' I ask, as she mutters 'Oh, for Christ's sake,' into air thick with other people's breath. On the stairwells, there are no windows to open. The green standby light gives her a sickly tinge. Ventilation is provided here and there by vents, but it isn't enough to quell the smell of bodies in over-exertion, packed tightly together.

She holds her hands out, as if to ask: is anyone alright?

'Do you know what happened?' I ask, as we start on yet another flight. My toes crush at the end of my boots. My shoulders scream at me.

'They sent us a message. The Power.' She frowns at me and I see in those tight brows that she is actually quite young, 'didn't you get it too?'

'I–' I grope around for an idea and as I do so, my bladder reminds me it is filling up, 'I was in the toilet when I heard all the noise. I sort of got… swept up.'

'Swept up in a revolution!' She laughs, 'In yet another exodus!'

It is my turn to frown at her, because I need her to confirm what I already know, I press her: 'What did the Power say?'

'That there is no more rain. That outside, it is safe.'

I look away from her, my cheeks hot.

'Then they quoted something from a book I've never heard of.'

Did I start a revolution?

*

My parents were quite traditional. They began to worry about me around the same time I began to worry about the planet. Dad hated the thought of me at protests. He believed I would meet the wrong sort of man. I met Henry, and to me he was just the right sort. Mum believed I shouldn't spend my weekends racing around the country 'complaining to the government', that I should have

101

a baby. I did have a baby. A baby that started coming with me to the protests, if we deemed it safe.

I tried to keep him safe always. That is the first and last line in a mother's contract, isn't it?

Both my parents wanted me to be a mum as a full-time job, even though my own mother had worked after having me. I followed in their footsteps, got good at IT, and spent days on end in cold humming rooms, sliding things in and out of server cabinets, fooling myself that certain lights were blinking a code to me.

A code that only I could decipher.

*

As the work gets harder, the crowd grows quieter. Frequently, I catch the eyes of those before and behind, as we turn to check we're not being followed. I assume, at first, that the guards are waiting at the bottom, ready to haul us all back to our quarters to sleep off this big stupid adventure, but as we get towards the lower levels, doors to the left of us open and other officials, higher ranking than me – I only know this because I've seen them close to the PM, their uniforms give nothing away – step into the throng. There are Scientists too! Their white coats reveal them. They have bags on their backs, and eyes straight ahead. No one says anything to them. We admit them into our desperate flow with indifference. I see P'tit and he seems even smaller now. I am tempted to call to him, but the stairwell echoes with steps and stomps, and I don't know his real name.

No one is talking. Some of us are scared, all of us excited. Many of us are tired to our very bones.

Some of us know what is coming next.

The ladder.

*

My parents died a decade ago, within a year of each other.

I became obsessed with a social simulation game. It took me from my own son, my own family life. Clém was older, less interested in Gaia and more so in his phone and friends at school. Henry treated me so carefully, let me do exactly what I wanted. In hindsight, it was kindness. At the time, it almost felt like indifference.

I spent my weekends bathed in the blue of a computer screen. The aim of the game was to create a happy life on a small, peaceful island. The island was tropical, the neon blue sea lapped at the bright yellow shore.

I created an avatar for mum and dad. I hacked it a bit, of course. Gave dad the moustache he had always wanted. Put framed photos of the three of us on holiday on the wall of their cottage. Designed a flowerbed in the shape of a rocket, a nod to their once successful careers.

The game followed my time zone – their night fell when mine did. When I woke in the morning, so did they.

I never did wrap the game up. They exist there, still.

I hope.

*

There is some panic when those at the front of the group, about a kilometre down, reach the western-most parapet. Movement slows, then stops. We are exhausted, we sit, slumped, on the stairs. The gloomy stairwell towers above us. It makes me dizzy to look up.

We are also anxious to carry on, before our legs seize up and stop working forever. Conversation starts again. I learn that the woman beside me is called Liesel, that she regrets ever coming up here in the first place.

'I want to take my chances with the world outside,' she explains. She doesn't ask me why I'm moving. I can't tell her about Clém, not about the dread, growing warmer within me, that he won't be waiting at the bottom of the ladder.

P'tit has disappeared ahead. Does he know it was me? Is he an accessory to the crime? Are we now... on the run?

*

Several years after the video game obsession,

three months into the time of non-stop rain,

before the first wave,

they took me up to the Tower.

They took me because I was good at my job.

They took me because I looked meek. I am meek, really. My voice has only ever been amplified by the louder people with whom I surround myself.

They took me because I could put up very little resistance, especially as the injection they gave me took hold.

They lay me out in the back of a truck and as I drifted off, all I could think was that I wouldn't be able to make the cake for Clem's twenty-fifth birthday, that coming weekend.

*

The ladder is awful. It is like the sort of theme park ride Henry or I would have to go on to keep Clém company. Vomit-inducing for anyone who chooses to look down. I am fortunate the Liesel is strong-stomached. I spend the hour it takes to climb down (arms burning, legs nothing but two pieces of string now) watching Liesel's plain black boots – Tower-issued, of course – step on the same rung where my fingers have just rested. There is a rhythm to it. A code.

White rung,
brown fingers,

103

black boots.
Clément, be there.

White rung,
brown fingers,
black boots.
Clément, I need you.

I can't hear anything but the clang of the metal ladder, the occasional whoosh of air that makes the tunnel shake a little. It lifts the smell of sweat from those below, the sour smell of fear, but beneath all those sickly top-notes, there is a smell of rotting leaves, of bird poo. Liesel can smell it too. In her heavy breathing, I can sense a smile.

Occasionally, I check on her. Rarely, she checks on me.

At one point, she says: 'No more rain?'

It is more a question than a statement.

'No more waves,' I respond, and then, as I begin to see daylight beneath my feet, I add: 'Renaissance.'

Our Land, Our Rules

Election day dawns damp. I can hear the rain falling on the corrugated roof of my hut. Argos pushes her warm wiry back into my middle, not quite ready for me to stir yet. I look across at Troy. His eyes are wide open and there is a sheen over the deep brown – he has barely slept. I could ask him what is on his mind, but I don't want to force him to lie.

I kiss Argos right between her ears and force myself out of bed. I pull on a t-shirt and some shorts. The day is warm and humid when I step out. The fire from last night still steams in the middle of our plot. Argos, apparently reluctant to stay with my uneasy bedfellow, follows me out. She bows in a stretch to the new day. She wants breakfast.

*

Liesel appears while I am watching the dogs eat. There are about six regulars now, I've got no clue what happened to the rest of them. Scattered across the county maybe. I picture a kind of peaceful species-ism – the Greyhounds have found the best place for haring, the Terriers have found the rattiest hide-outs, the Labs have found the sea. I haven't been to the coast for years. The North Sea, with all its unpredictability, fills me with fear. I am dizzy, busy imagining the waves, when she comes up to me. I don't hear her footsteps over the clamour of the dog bowls knocking together, over the swish of their wagging tails and their delighted grunts.

'Is he in there?' she asks, nodding towards my hut. She is everything I would have found terrifying Before. She is comfortable in her long, strong body. A statue of hard-wearing femininity. The old me would have run for the trees, would have gone mad with jealousy over Troy.

The new me tries their best to smile at her: 'Yes, and he's awake, if you want to see him.'

She frowns at me. I feel just brave enough to take her in. She really is quite beautiful. Cropped auburn hair falling onto delicate, freckled cheekbones. Eyes the colour of fresh laurel.

'A-are you sure?'

I shrug. 'You two must have a lot to catch up on.'

Liesel takes a deep breath, and I can hear tears in her throat. She puts her hands on her hips, turns towards the Tower.

'I don't know where to start,' she begins, dropping to her haunches and putting her hand out as the Dalmatian – she always finishes first – comes up to

105

her. Before fully committing, the dog looks at me.

'Good girl,' I say. 'She's safe.'

The dog begins to nuzzle at Liesel's hands with gusto. I can feel Liesel's eyes on me, but I only have so much in my kindness tank and I'm drained of courage. Talking to her about how she should begin again with Troy, the partner she left to 'save herself' in the Tower, would empty me completely.

'Does he…' she begins, her face buried deep in spotted black and white fur, 'did he ever mention me?'

'Nope.' I move over to the fire, Argos at my heels, and begin to build it for the day's ceremonies. Under the leaves of the trees, it is protected enough to stay lit, as long as there isn't a huge downpour. Argos starts seeking small twigs for kindling in the undergrowth behind Troy's hut. I look back at Liesel and realise she's crying.

'But don't take it personally. It is a rule here. No talking about Before.'

'Your lot have a lot of rules.'

'We do. They've worked so far.'

'We'll see.'

Having got what she wanted, Liesel stands and wipes off the dog hairs from her jeans. She looks at my hut and then at me.

'I'll wait for tonight's results,' she explains, to no one in particular, before picking her way delicately past the remnants of the feeding line and down towards the new camp, which nestles into the hillside below us. A dangerous choice, in the rain.

'Watch out for the hogweed!' I shout after her because, even though she is the enemy, she should know that the glorious, umbrella-sized heads of white flowers to her left are incredibly poisonous. The weed is bigger this year than it ever has been, and I want her to lose in a fair fight against Martha, not to fall out of the race because she is covered head to toe in blisters.

She points to the plant beside her: 'But that's cow parsley!'

I shake my head. 'Believe me, it isn't what you think it is!'

Argos barks her agreement.

*

Everyone is very quiet over breakfast. Martha especially. Her shoulders, normally squared and braced to all weathers, roll forward in the mist that has followed the early morning rain. Today is one of those days where her wheelchair wants to swallow her whole. Aleks keeps smiling at her, but she doesn't seem interested. She must be nervous about the speech and the vote.

Troy sits close to me, perhaps to ease his inner turmoil. Argos growls at him, but I shoo her away. When I give his hand a squeeze, he looks like he might cry, so I stop touching him and focus on my porridge.

There are no Tower plans for the day. Not only is it Election Day, but

Graham, our drunken former architect, doesn't think the Tower is safe to visit right now. We wouldn't be able to slip up there unnoticed and we'd be mobbed for the contraband we're carrying. We've already had to seek out some stronger padlocks for our warehouses.

'Stick to feeding the refugees at the base,' Martha tells us all, 'be nice to them. We don't want to attract the attention of The Hand.'

The Tower's inhabitants – the Dwellers – are pouring out of it. Hundreds a day. They spend a night recovering at the foot of the leg, their descent stripping them of energy. Aleks, Troy, Graham and I take it in turns, as pairs, to feed them, to keep them warm and if possible, dry.

When they're strong enough, they disperse across the county – some to the coast, some to the Cheviots, some to towns and cities which probably no longer exist, due to the flooding.

Some are looking for the homes we've looted and searched. They're desperate to start over again, to return to normal life. To forget this slight blip in their years on earth. Like Liesel.

Others have gone half-mad and as soon as their legs work again, they just run, their lungs full of sweet, un-filtered air.

With no access to information, we can't figure out what suddenly changed, why the sudden Exodus. The Dwellers won't tell us anything, still scared of incurring the wrath of the regime they have left behind, but for a month or so now, we've heard a constant rustle in the undergrowth, a continuous beat of footfall.

Dwellers pass through here every day. Pale, shorn. Eyes blinking in the brightness of the world, in teary surprise that people have survived and are ruddy with health. Advertisements, we are, for the glory of the Outside, proof that the government lied to them about the trouble that lay ahead, down here. That they continued the lie, up there. Martha's rule: we don't read the National Press here. Nothing government-controlled could be credible, but even strict Martha can fall victim to vanity – we did let them interview us. One of their bright young journalists – Hannah May – came sniffing around. Martha thought it best to put across our side of the story. So, we told her everything. In return, she told us that Middlesbrough was now almost entirely underwater.

Somehow, we got hold of the article in print. Martha read it once, then used it to start a fire. We don't need to know what is going on outside of the allotment.

As Martha says, all we need is to put our trust in the spring of the grass and the sturdiness of tree trunks.

I put my faith in the pad of a soft paw, or how the sunlight occasionally catches the slope of the back of a dog, mid-stretch.

Recently, the camp where Liesel first pitched up has grown. She too has become a leader of sorts. She stands on stones and declares new ideas to her camp of followers, her mustard coloured t-shirt rippling in the breeze. A modern-day Boudicca.

But she's no Martha.

*

Martha has us all seated around her. The Dwellers and Graham, Aleks, Troy and me. Argos curls into the space between my crossed legs. In the crepuscular firelight, Martha's chin juts forward: she is glorious, strong. She has plaited some couch grass with mares-tail for a headdress – a thing of beauty made from weeds. It is cleverly symbolic, and we can all see how it makes Liesel's eyes twitch.

'Thank you all for being here,' Martha begins, and we all look around at each other. I am seated beside a teenage Dweller, whose hair is too short and body too angular to gender. I grin at them. They look me up and down with a surprised eyebrow – and then grin back.

'It is a joy to see so many Tower citizens reclaiming their right to the earth.'

There is a small smattering of applause. I look at Liesel, who is standing on the edge of the circle, near my hut, her eyes fixed on Martha. I look at Troy sitting beside me – he is looking down at his hands.

They really need to talk.

'And this is our earth. This is where we come from, where we will end. Our blood is made from this soil, our past is written on its trees, our future in the seeds working hard beneath our feet.'

She takes a quick breath. 'This is where we belong. This is our home. We are responsible for it and it, in its wisdom, has given us a second chance. My proposal is that we take this opportunity, that we grab it with both hands. We don't get ahead of ourselves, not again. We go back to basics!'

Graham and Aleks cheer. I wonder if Martha asked them to.

'Back to farming our land as it was farmed before the machine-loving-animal-haters took over. Back to the simple things, like campfires and days off on Sundays and natural remedies for the things that ail us.'

I look at Martha's skinny legs beneath her strong torso.

Argos lets out a soft, low whine.

'In short, my people,' Martha says, slowly drawing a theatrical hand across the rapt crowd, 'let us not forget our history, but learn from it. Let us take advantage of the second chance we've been given and raise a new green and pleasant land.'

There is applause from many of us, including the Dwellers. A few die-hard Liesel fans sit with their arms crossed – you can't win them all, Martha, but all you have to do is win enough of them.

Aleks stands and wheels Martha down the ramp of logs that Troy and I spent the afternoon securing. It had been good to work with him in the warmth of the day, to feel his arm strong against mine. I look at him again and I see that he is looking at me, all his features soft.

Liesel takes to the stage. She has no head adornment, no special look to sell us. Perhaps she doesn't need it. If Martha looked strong, Liesel looks like a demi-god. Her arms, fists clenched, ripple with anticipation of the fight. I look back at Troy again, but he is transfixed.

'Thank you so much, Martha. Your speech was very… wistful. There is so much sentiment in it that I agree with. And may I just say – it is such a pleasure to be standing in the same spot where, only a few years ago, my fiancé Troy and I, shared an allotment,' Liesel starts, gesturing towards us. I take one of Argos's paws, hold it tight. The dog's wet nose finds the crook at my knee. 'And we did just that – share. We knew, even as we planned and sowed and harvested, that the land we worked was only ever borrowed.'

Graham mutters something under his breath, but Martha, her arms neatly in her lap, shushes him with a slight smile.

'Ownership is not the answer. Stewardship is.' Liesel raises her eyes to the sky, as if overwhelmed by everything and then stares hard into the crowd. 'The question I want to ask you is what do you want to pass on? What legacy do you want to leave behind?'

The Dwellers whisper to each other. The positive susurration makes me nervous.

'Do we want to forget everything we've learnt from our work in the Tower? From the Greenhouses and the laboratories? From the Scientists?'

There is a sharp intake of breath. A collective shiver.

'We cannot forget what we have been through,' Liesel soldiers on, despite the less boisterous reception. 'But we can glean goodness from it – just as you can make compost from waste. Or indeed, grow sustenance from manure.'

I see Troy nod beside me. I see him smile at Liesel.

What flowers can I grow from this shit?

'Choosing me as your leader will be a choice for progress. For using the old to bring in the new. For Renaissance.' Liesel pauses, theatrically, 'For going forwards, not backwards.'

'To going forwards!' cries Troy, causing Argos to leap from her leg-nest and growl at him. Despite Troy's obvious adoration, the applause is not equal to Martha's. Something about Liesel's words and the way she holds herself, waving at the crowd, as she descends, reminds me too much of the last lot of politicians, the ones who put us here in the first place. Some fans throw flowers at Liesel as she walks towards the Dwellers' side of the camp. Someone has snipped some marigolds from somewhere and there are one or two sunflowers that they must have taken from Graham's patch. I am looking at Troy when I hear Liesel scream. I see his face contort and harden. I see him unfold and lunge towards her as she crumples to her knees, clutching her face.

*

Despite the hogweed attack and what I can only imagine were a few sympathy votes, Martha wins. We use weeds so as not to waste paper. Mares tail for Martha, docks for Liesel. Aleks counts and Troy double-checks. They both have skin in the game, so it seems the most trustworthy way to do it. I watch my two friends counting together, their spines just visible beneath the hardened wall of their combined backs. When they finish, they hug, and I feel a small pinch of jealousy.

Troy returns to Liesel's blistered side, working hard not to catch my eye. One of Liesel's lids is swollen shut, but we think she's been spared blindness, thanks to Troy's quick actions with the water butt. The poison has, if anything, made her face more interesting. Battle scars are, after all, part and parcel of this life we now lead.

*

'We need to educate the Dwellers,' Martha says, that night. Aleks, Graham, Argos and I sit at her feet by the fire. 'The hogweed incident has made that blindingly obvious.'

Graham chuckles. We all clutch a beaker of his cider in celebration of Martha's – of our – success.

'Robin would be good at that.' Aleks is being over-kind to me, to compensate for the lack of Troy. I am sturdy enough without him, I hope.

'I agree,' Martha says, her voice quiet. She must be exhausted. She looks at me.

'Robin, I am sure Troy will come back when he and Liesel have discussed ev–'

I shake my head, look over to my hut which I know is empty. I stand up, wiping my shorts free of earth. Argos is on her paws, looking up at me too. I hold my cup out.

A smile comes easily, on a dry warm night full of victory.

'Our land, our rules!' I cry into the canopy above us.

Happy Anniversary

They come down off the tower with the fourth wave of Dwellers. They don't leave with the first waves because they need time to prepare, to try to get everything back. How much of what they came with could they bear to leave behind?

Lloyd is a wreck when they meet in their planned spot, at the planned time. His arms are empty.

'Zaha is alive.' He takes huge gulps of the stale, recycled air. 'But they threatened to kill me if I tried to take her.'

'She's safe,' Rhona says, not recognising her own cold voice. 'We don't know what it is like out there.' Her throat already aches from all the talking she's not used to doing.

'I told them, I told her, we'll come back for her.' Lloyd can hear the falseness of the words, remembering the scorn on the face of the Scientist holding the hand of a confused Zaha, holding his daughter, who had no clue who he was.

'We will come back, when we're set up.'

'Of course, we will,' Rhona agreed.

*

The descent from their sector itself takes a dizzying three hours, down a chilly stairwell with no windows. They pause more and more frequently to catch their breath. He retches once, she a few times. The last stage is spent shimmying down a rickety ladder in the western-most Leg.

Her arms ache from gripping too tightly. Her weakened legs slip and skim the rungs.

She has never liked heights. One half of an architect super-couple who specialised in skyscrapers. She prefers to look up at the irony, rather than down from it.

At the bottom of the Leg, they collapse on the sun-warmed soil, altering their breathing, waiting for the necessary physical adjustments to occur. Their senses, numbed for so long by life in the Tower, begin to wake up. The fresh air is delicious. It smells like rosehips and hot beaten earth. They take in huge chunks of it with great, laughter-filled inhalations.

Then Rhona tries to stand.

Her legs refuse.

Lloyd wobbles around for a step or two and then lands beside her with a thud.

She prods the muscles above her knees. He rubs his lower legs, feeling flesh popping and bubbling beneath the surface. She tells her brain to move her feet. It is no use.

'We're not in any hurry,' Lloyd says, the twist in his mouth confirming he is lying.

They remain stuck there in the beautiful sunshine. Other Dwellers crash around them. Their closeness is both comforting and unwanted. The architects, the vanguard trying to flee from their self-made, self-designed prison, couldn't get away quickly enough.

In time, people from the allotments emerge from the undergrowth and offer them sustenance in the form of out-of-date juice cartons and chocolate bars that have been melted and reformed.

'They're the ones,' Rhona tells Lloyd, nodding to a compact young man… or woman… (she can't really tell) who continues down the line of Dwellers offering food and drink. A chestnut-coloured mongrel trots along beside the donor, accepting the occasional ear ruffle from the delighted, exhausted refugees.

Lloyd looks at her, sweat beading on his high forehead. He raises an eyebrow.

'The contraband,' she whispers, then remembers she doesn't need to be quiet anymore. 'They're the ones who took our letters.'

*

They end up sleeping at the base of the Tower. By the time they can even consider moving, gnats are beginning to swarm. Somewhere over the hill, there is a thunder of barking and yowling as the allotment dogs are fed their dinner.

They are not the only ones. Once again, another pair of allotment people emerge with blankets and a motley selection of pilfered, second-hand camping equipment.

'You are welcome to join us for food,' the owner of the mongrel is back, a smile on their face.

Rhona, lying on her back in the soft, sweet grass, doesn't reply. Lloyd declines for both of them. Instead, he covers Rhona's deep breathing form with a blanket. He puts his back to her and curls up. It has been a lifetime since they slept beside each other. And although the night is starry, and the wood smoke from the various allotment fires lends the air all the nostalgia it could hold, and although they are free… Lloyd can't bear to touch Rhona, not yet.

As the night creeps in, and things go still and quiet, he keeps Zaha in his mind, sealing her in his memory. He does not give in to sleep.

*

The next morning, they set out as soon as it is light. The allotment people give them cereal bars that are only a year and a half out of date.

'Hardly a continental breakfast,' Lloyd attempts to joke.

'It'll do,' Rhona grouches, her whole body humming with the pain of yesterday's descent.

112

Their path of escape wends its way through the rest of the allotment, the place where the Exodus started. The people who showed them life still went on, on the Outside.

Everywhere they look, there are welcome and definite signs of care, new-looking warehouses, smoke from dampened fires. They pass through tent cities, people with lengthening hair and dirty feet beckon to them as they go by.

Now that Rhona's legs work, and heavy with the knowledge that Zaha remains in the Tower and their future together as a safe, happy family remains unsecured; stopping is more than either of them can bear to think about.

*

Lloyd and Rhona are heading west. Inland. At first, they had considered a scenic route along the Tyne, but as they neared Fenham, they saw that this would be impossible. Scotswood Road, with its industrial estates and car dealerships, was gone. Entirely under water. What had once been an industrially evocative view of Newcastle's former glory was now one big puddle.

'This is unprecedented,' Lloyd says, looking at Rhona for an explanation she can't give.

'Our house is underwater,' she replies, looking to the south east.

*

Inland, onward.

They take the main road west, the flooded river – the wetlands – to the south of them. The A69 is mainly quiet, at first. As are they. There is just the occasional speck of a person in the distance, a fire, discarded rubbish. They walk past two empty cabins that were according to the stamp of the crown on the outside – old checkpoints.

'They said that there were officers everywhere, down here,' Lloyd frowns. Rhona looks into the cabin as they pass it.

'They've jumped ship,' she surmises.

Then, before their eyes, a long line of Dwellers sprouts up.

'They must be coming up from the south,' Lloyd says, as they march almost silently past them, not looking left or right.

'They look exhausted,' Rhona says. 'How long do you think they've been travelling?'

At the rear of the long line of people, a statuesque woman dressed in bright colours beams at them.

'You're going the wrong way, my friends,' she says, teeth white, brown skin shining. 'Redemption can be found beside the North Sea.'

At the thought of all that water, Lloyd seeks Rhona's hand. It has been some time since he has held her hand. She blinks and sees the bodies of hundreds of dead birds. He blinks and hears the roar of a freak wave, bearing down on them.

Both of them shudder, wish the woman well. They begin to walk again, their very bones creaking like old, underused pistons.

The hedgerows and verges are reclaiming space, teeming with late summer wasps.

The hot tarmac gives Lloyd a constant sweaty sheen.

Both of them feel the air on their entwined fingertips, too overwhelmed to speak.

*

When they reach the outskirts of Hexham, night is falling. They find a disused stable in a field and decide it will have to do.

At least it is high and dry, Rhona says.

Lloyd spreads out the thin coverlets they took from the Tower, packed hastily into matching backpacks. Just outside the hut, they make a fire with matches from the people at the allotment. Lloyd sits there, watching the flames dance, drinking some of the liquid dinner, the protein gloop, they stole on their way down from the Tower.

'Look what I have.' Rhona produces a brown bottle. It is no longer than the palm of her hand in which it rests. It is the colour of wheat as it starts to rot. His face twists.

'Is that...?'

She nods. 'It is, I've kept it. All this time.'

He doesn't know what to say. She is so proud of herself, he recognises that in her small smile as she lowers herself to sit beside him. An almost-grimace, as gravity and the wear and tear of their second day Outside take hold. Still, it is worth it for the view. Their hilltop field gives way to dusky, rewilded farmland. Things rustle and wave.

Rhona looks like she did when they first met, over a decade ago. Time rewinds in a moment. There that girl is, her face held so close to his, at the entrance to the Metro station. She's older, of course, but she's still the reflection of whatever goodness she saw in him.

'I thought, since it was the anniversary, and all.'

Today, the day on which they left, is the anniversary of their entrance to the Tower.

Just five years ago. Five years since they have shared a living space, a bed. Not that that always stopped them. They found secret spaces, when they felt brave enough. And, if there were prying eyes, they were willing to be blind. To concede to the 'special couple' some privacy in their togetherness. They'd be foolish to think that their liaisons went unnoticed. Everything was monitored in the Tower, from toilet paper usage to how late you kept your light on.

Lloyd seeks her hand. His fingers are inky with past ideas.

114

'Still working?' She frowns down at them, rubbing at the pen stains.

Rhona is jealous, he realises, she must think that he found time, in all the existing, to create. He shakes his head. 'Architect's block, I'm afraid.' He gestures to the Tower that hangs behind them like a storm. 'I feel like we peaked somewhat, don't you? Creating anything else seems–'

'Greedy?'

'That's the one. Greedy.'

Something squeaks, another something howls. Catching their breath from the surprise, they take in the lively hedgerow before them, gloomy in the dusk. It seems to be the stage for an intense battle.

'Of course, I couldn't design more without you.'

Her lips draw together. She blinks a few times and then holds her chin up to the firelight. He studies the familiar face with renewed angst. Her strange, short haircut makes her look the sort of feral he feels she'd always wanted to be, deep down.

She detaches and reaches into the pocket of her blue oilskin. The one she the Scientist provided her with in the never-ending downpour that drove them to the Tower. It goes so well with the bright yellow of his. Another one of their clever architect ideas. A way of sorting the Dwellers before they even climbed the ladders. Tower swag, Tower stash. A waste of money, in a building entirely closed to the elements. Still, he tells himself, the colour combo is one thing of beauty to be found in their five-year-long segregation.

We brought this on ourselves, he thinks.

'Come on.' She shakes her shoulders free of the phantom hair that once was. 'I've bought glasses and everything.'

She pulls out a pair of the type of glasses they used to give away free at distillery tours. A bell shape, most of the lettering scraped off, but shiny clean. In the funny games memory plays, he sees the stormy roll of the southern Hebrides and her face superimposed on a backdrop of threatening sky.

'How on earth did you…?'

'I found them actually, the other day. In a roll of socks,' she shrugs. 'I must have thought them important when we had to leave, that night.'

She remembers hard wood floors and detailed banisters. Shot glasses in a cupboard. A cat asleep on a pile of blueprints. Her daughter gurgling beside her in the highchair.

His laugh, like a bark, hurls her back whole eras to the morning he first stayed over, and she offered to cook him the only warm breakfast she knew how to make – porridge.

'Why did you wait to show me?' He is thinking aloud. Her face falls, so he turns towards her. 'S-sorry, that sounded ungrateful, I just meant…'

'Zaha. She'll have turned five recently.'

They both stare into the bushes and instead see their daughter, barely a year old, wrapped in the green oilskin that would define her as Generation B. Surrounded by other babies in green oilskins. An uncertain smile on her soft sleeping face, a look of steel on the face of the Scientist who held her.

'You know, give it another century, and the Tower will be peat,' Rhona coughs the emotion from her voice. 'Maybe the Scientists will start their own distillery.'

'Name it after us, do you think? Another legacy for us to uphold?'

It is her turn to laugh, and his to miss her, even though she is right beside him.

'We'll be long gone by then. And our whole generation! Burnt and tossed over the edge, like they all are.'

He thinks: *architects used to be buried at the base of their creations.*

He doesn't want to be buried.

He looks at his blue-marked fingers again.

She thinks: *you could argue that we found the solution too late. That the huge complex we designed, with its manifold floors and colour-coded sectors, only shelters the doomed.*

And that the people who are really to blame – those that could have found a true solution - are already buried far beneath.

They both think: *we are built on bodies. We have built on bodies.*

'Fill her up.' Lloyd holds out both their glasses and she breaks the seal on the bottle. A sudden wind threatens to whip the liquid away, so they huddle. They breathe peat and smoke and each other.

'Cheers!'

She takes a sip. It burns all the way down.

Her island's life blood.

He breathes out, letting the smoked taste trickle down his nostrils. He coughs.

'Good, isn't it?' She smiles sleepily at him.

He nods.

Just one taste and he is transported back there, to her island. There he is, slipping in the mud, clinging to her and to fences.

Now he is sliding about happily in what is left of the bogs.

And here is that cup of tea by the fireside with a good book or even a crappy DVD at the end of another day of peat-digging.

And there he is, in the car beside her, as she takes, at an unnerving pace, those terrible rutted roads where both the corners and the rabbits are blind.

116

'We never did name it.' Rhona burps slightly as the liquid sets its burning course down her throat.

It is night dark now. Soon, they'll get to curl up beside each other for the first time in five years (last night's weary paralysis didn't count, in Rhona's opinion).

He doesn't want to argue, not now.

She says: 'Zaha came along so soon after.'

They both look at the vegetation in front of them, their eyes narrowed.

He says: 'Tell me a story.'

She thinks of bedtimes and tartan bedspreads and the warmth of a small body beside her. She takes a deep breath, allowing her natural theatricality to mask it all.

'Once upon a time,' she starts, and he snorts into his glass. 'Before distilleries were legal, they would hide the stills from the taxmen. They'd see them coming across the water–' she waves her hand at the dark shapes of hedge in front of them and it becomes a shared maritime mirage, complete with a small yet officious looking boat, 'and they would ring an emergency bell.'

He taps his glass with his fingernail and it rings out over the darkening hilltop.

'On hearing the bell the brewers – monks probably – would rush to hide the stills.' She pauses. Her face is full of a bad memory. He looks away.

'Where would they hide them?' He asks, holding out his empty glass because the bottle was there to be finished, as her brother used to say. She moves onto her knees, tops them both up.

'In coffins.' She settles back beside him. 'They'd rush them up to the local church–'

'The stills?'

'Of course, they were smaller in those days. Small enough to be carried by a quick child.' A gulp.

They had failed as parents by succeeding as architects. They had been unable to carry her up to their well-designed, segregated quarters, when the separating happened. She was to stay down in green, with the other children. Far from blue. Furthest from yellow.

And if they didn't get her back, she would be brought up as a generation ignorant of the world that stretched at their feet right now.

Generation B.

He thought: *the next generation has to forget what has come before in order to create what will come next.*

She thought: *in theory, yes, but what about in practice?*

'So… the stills?' He nudges her on the elbow and feels the chill on her skin.

He moves closer to her. She shifts towards him.

'Yes, the stills. They'd put them in coffins, place the coffins ceremoniously about and by the time Mr Tax Man arrived, he would have to console them for the town's loss. He'd pay his respects and then head on up the coast to the next distillery, which was probably doing the exact same thing.'

He shakes his head in glee at the story.

'I can't believe I've never heard that one!'

'I'm full of surprises today.'

He kisses her cheek swiftly.

*

It begins to drizzle. The fire spits. Rhona raises her chin, accepts the rain as a plant would.

Lloyd says, 'It is getting late.'

He stands, his bottom numb from the earth and his head liquid from the drink. He offers his hand to her and she takes it. Once up, she presses his knuckles to her lips and breathes in deeply.

She asks, 'Do you think we'll make it?'

He nods, 'All we need to do is head up, and West.'

Away from the coast, she thinks.

Avoid the waves, he thinks.

'At least we're not driving,' she smiles. 'Remember driving on a hangover?'

'Like the good old peat days,' he laughs. She tucks her hands under her armpits.

'Shall we?' He gestures towards the stable. She nods and turns away from him. Then after a couple of steps, she pauses. She looks back at the dark hillside, hears the hoot of an owl. He watches her, her body still a straight line, unbent by the wind.

'We'll go back for her,' she tells him.

'Of course we will,' he replies.

Benthesikyme Styx

A trickle of Dwellers becomes a stream, a river becomes a wave. Constant movement, from the break of day to the last light of dusk.

No, hyperbolic. Try it another way.

Hundreds of Dwellers are leaving the Towers daily. Although they don't seem to be travelling at night, these early autumn days are long for them, weighed down with –

You're doing it again. You can't write worth shit.

A day in the life of a typical Dweller.
Get up, descend thousands of stairs, blink in the bright sunlight that hasn't touched your skin in months, start to move. Keep on moving.

What are you doing, labelling them? Rendering them faceless, characterless? These are scared people, who have been duped by countless uninformed governments and possibly poisoned (not enough research on that yet. It is so hard to get any information without running it past the interim government).

Drugged, at least. You know yourself that when you picture a Dweller, you see a very specific face.

And there goes your phone again, always vibrating across the desk, or the dinner table, or the mattress, regardless of the hour. Chris'll get angry, if she hears you're still up and working for the government. Not that she should be angry – you're both allowed a phone because of this job. And you did all that paperwork to apply for them, for the both of you. After all, this job has kept you financially safe, semi-furloughed for the past few years, while the dust settled. She should be grateful.

…

But she's not here to be angry, or grateful, is she?

An email, from the big boss:
To: h.may@freshstartmag.np.uk
From: j.strickland@freshstartmag.np.uk
Subject: Think Piece

119

Dear Hannah,
I hope this finds you well and at peace.

You know it is code, but you still hate that phrase. You are certainly not at peace, but Jaimini has to write this, to let you know that whatever you read next is coming from the top. Not just from her, but from the Power, your guardians for the past five years, since the Tower shot up and you lost the Lottery. Kept the wolf from the door (in some respects) and stopped you developing too strong a love for the pastoral and joining one of those allotment cults.

Emily suggested you are currently at a bit of a loose end

Cheers, Emily. Some office friend she is.

and she also mentioned your connection to the Towers

Fred... you would be furious at Emily, if you didn't suspect that the government knew all about you, anyway

so I have a job for you.

You're relieved, aren't you? You should be. Something else to focus on other than the sound of Boatswain licking his bits on the bed behind you, his canine cleanliness an echoing reminder of how empty your life has suddenly become.
So, Strickland, what have you got?

There is a new 'Dweller' leader, sees herself as a bit of a messiah – one Benthesikyme Styx.

What a name! Benthe-si-kym-e? and Styx – imagine the headlines that could be written with that name!

We think that she needs investigating.

Jaimini only says 'we' when she means the ones in charge. It must be galling for her, once such a renowned reporter, to have to kowtow to the government.
You, on the other hand, are quite happy to sell your soul, as long as you're allowed to keep writing, to keep your job.

She seems to think that everyone who is leaving a tower needs to move to water.

She predicts a huge wave (!) and that those who survive the wave will be reborn (!!) A holy-water type thing, I guess.

A prisoner of the Tower gone mad, type thing, you guess.

We want to know if she's telling the truth.

In other words, the big bosses want to know if she's dangerous to your, and their, precarious existence. And if she is, they want to deal with her.

Apparently, she's making her way up from Middlesbrough. Sources say that it is almost uninhabitable now.

Such a knowledgeable woman, your boss. Facts at her fingertips.

And is leading her 'people' north-east, to the coast. Or what's left of it. Right through Newcastle. I thought you might like to join the crowd for a few days, see if you can document the movement.

It is appealing, you can't deny it. Surrounding yourself with a bunch of weirdos for a few days might make you forget about Chris and Fred for a bit.

There seem to be quite a lot of 'new religions' popping up all over the country at the moment

You think of Chris and her odd behaviour lately. Outings late at night and early in the morning. Refusal to use her phone for calls. As if afraid that they are listening to her. Admittedly, a justified fear.

and, well, your piece on the eco-fascism of post-Tower allotments went viral, so I thought you might be interested.

That is the closest Strickland gets to a compliment. Well done to you. It was a good piece, you have to admit. The mag even said they'd pay for you to travel to the States and find out more about the 'Land Reclaimers', who are rising up on the west coast islands created by the sea-level rise.
When you're allowed to travel again.
If you're allowed to travel again.
And of course, if the rumours are true, the Power always know more than they're letting on.

121

You and Fred were such good travel buddies. It didn't matter where dad stuffed you (in the back of a small car, sharing a train seat, on his knee on National Express), you'd always make the best of it. Your dad loved trains, didn't he?

Read on Hannah, quickly –

Let me know what you think – but do get back to me ASAP, Hannah. They'll be passing through the day after tomorrow and we'll need to sort out security (!) and check the weather report (!!). Don't think you want to go into battle with a freak 'moral' wave.

Ouch. What does she mean by that?

*

Boatswain, Hannah tells herself, *focus on Boatswain.* He is all tail-wags and jaunty paws at the first sniff of adventure. And she would be normally, were it not for Chris. This is the first time Hannah will leave the flat for more than a quick dog walk since she went away.

But Chris isn't some lost puppy. She knows where home is.

She's more like a cat, Hannah thinks angrily. *This home isn't suitable for her anymore. She can get tastier cream elsewhere.*

Cream that hasn't, in Chris's words, 'sold out',

Boatswain loves it when Hannah packs, until the idea that he might not be coming with her enters his tiny, perfect brain. Then his ears go so far to the back of his head he looks like a seal pup who's lost his colony.

'It's okay, buddy,' she reassures him, while shoving another pair of pants into her backpack. She has spent the last hour looking for the tent, but it is gone. Perhaps she binned it, or Chris did. She will have to take her chances, or ask Strickland to get one to her. 'You're coming with us. With me.' A single swish of the tail. 'We're going to the beach,' she tells him, as he hops up onto her bed and settles down for the night, a fuzzy doughnut of wolf-like proportions. 'Eventually.'

Hannah has heard that at some of the more renowned beaches, almost all the sand has disappeared, that the dunes are riddled with new sink holes and quicksand, that those who didn't make it to the Towers are now fleeing inland and into the hills.

While the dog snores, she lies on her back, picking at the quicks around her nails. She thinks about what she's packed, whether she's got enough pens and paper, if she's charged enough battery packs to see her through.

She's not going to sleep, and she realises this three minutes into the night, so she hangs there in the darkness and imagines huge waves hitting the remains of the rugged Northumberland coast. Castles split in two, the ice-cream shops that she and Fred favoured as kids, obliterated. The poor, pixelated picture of Benthesikyme Styx that Strickland had attached to the email dances across her vision, cackling like the wicked witch of Middlesbrough, as seawater bores a hole through the eye sockets of her less worthy followers.

Hannah wakes up covered in sweat. Salty and tacky, she feels like her younger self, knackered after a day at the seaside.

Raindrops decorate the windows. In the grey and insipid dawn, Hannah scrawls a note to Chris, but her brain isn't fired up enough to make the perfect pun about waving goodbye, so instead she writes:

Strickland got me a job.
I love you.
I'll be home soon.

When he hears his lead, Boatswain skitters with joy, all the way to the door.

*

Fred always wanted a puppy, when you were kids. You were less keen, because you were the more responsible one and knew you'd be lumped with its care, but at night, in the bunkbed above you, he'd whisper into the darkness about all the adventures the two of you could have with a dog. His enthusiasm convinced you, as it always did when you were young. You battled and bartered with your dad, but he wasn't having any of it. Wasn't he doing enough, raising twins by himself with a full-time job in parliament, and a crazy mother-in-law?

You got upset whenever he called your grandmother crazy, but even your tears wouldn't convince him to get a dog.

Fred got Boatswain straight out of college. When Boatswain was a pup, Fred took him everywhere, even to job interviews. When he eventually got hired onto his apprenticeship, Boatswain learnt to be without him for six hours a day. He coped pretty well, but only because you lived close enough to pop over at lunch to let him out for a wee and give him some peanut butter on a cracker.

When Fred got the job on the rigs, the money was too good to turn down. Too good to question the drilling of the sea, the pillaging of resources, the care of his favoured pooch.

Of course, you took Boatswain in. Who else would have had him? (Probably a lot of people, actually, but you weren't willing to part with him.)

Somewhere in the middle of the North Sea, Fred got used to living high up, on his own, without his dog.

*

123

Hannah finds them along the A1, just past Gosforth. She can hear them. They aren't really loud, not yet. They're still on Tower mode, the human version of energy-saving light bulbs. They talk, but at a volume that barely rises above the sound of their feet shuffling on the tarmac. It makes her skin itch. Their combined sound is like a singer with their mic switched off, trying to lift their voice over the noise of the band. It irritates her.

She needs to stop calling them 'they' and 'them', and learn some names, meet some people. Boatswain looks up to her – and at her – for instructions on how to behave around these musty, sad people. Their shoulders sag with the realisation that they have been duped, that those in power at the time had sent them scurrying away from their homes to achieve a survival that had stopped life being worth living.

Or so Hannah used to say, before she realised that the government was always listening. And it swirled her messy insides up even more to think like that, when she knew Fred was in one of those towers, somewhere.

*

When Hannah first sees the line of angular, sharp bodies, swathed in too-big raincoats in blue and yellow, she stops. She hasn't seen so many people in one place for years, and the quantity, and their vicinity, brings breakfast to her throat. Boatswain lets out a slight whimper. She ruffles an ear, glad for his presence.

Deep down in the depths of Hannah's memory, there are snapshots of protests she went on. Officially, she atoned for them all, in writing, to secure her job with National Press. Chris was outraged, of course. This wasn't the Hannah she knew, the Hannah she had met, hair bright blue, at one of the protests following Britain's withdrawal from the Paris Agreement.

But Hannah was scared of rocking the boat, of upsetting the Hand – well the Power, really. A sign of weakness, according to Chris.

Hannah remembers too, all the concerts she enjoyed and reviewed, the clubs she danced in, where bodies of all shapes and sizes pressed sweatily against her. It was normal, then.

She forces herself to remember how she used to pick people out of a crowd in those days. She scans the line of Dwellers for a familiar yellow tuft of hair, but it is drizzling, there are hoods up. She wouldn't know Fred now, not just from a gait or a shoulder.

As the crowd walks past her, they don't look right or left. Most of them have their eyes fixed on the sky and miss Hannah's existence entirely. Exhaustion, Hannah assumes. Now that the bridges across the Tyne are all gone, many of them must have had to take the long way around to make it this far.

Now and then, a thin face glances back, the whites of eyes glow as they fixate on the Tower at their back. Hannah looks at it occasionally too, but she's used to seeing it, and feeling its shadow across the islands and lakes that now cover the south east of the city.

Hannah never did see inside. She didn't win the Lottery, and she had Chris, who wanted to see how it would all play out, outside.

She reminds herself that these people know more than she does, and have knowledge to share.

Hannah and Boatswain fall into step beside a small woman, perhaps younger than her, who walks beside a much taller and older man. They're bowed, their folded bodies equally braced against the wind coming off the water. Their cheeks are red with exertion – the veins in the man's jowls are exacerbated by his huge smile.

'It is so good to be outside,' he tells Hannah, gulping in huge breaths of the seaweed and sewage smell.

'There are still seagulls,' she tells Hannah, pointing up, her mouth so open in amazement that Hannah wants to tell her to be careful that one doesn't shit in it.

She asks them what happened that caused them to leave the quayside air, the gulls, and go to the Tower in the first place.

They give Hannah a bleary-eyed look she's seen before. For that renowned article that Strickland mentioned, Hannah visited a series of allotments. She interviewed a group of hippies. Chris calls them eco-fascists, but Hannah was slow to pass that judgement. She's had enough of terrorists to last her a lifetime.

The group leader was called Martha, and her face, in dappled sunlight, looked familiar to Hannah. She explained that her group had decided to stay behind as 'stewards' of what they believed to be a 'dying land'. She had introduced her to a Dweller, called Liesel, who was beautiful and scary and not the type of woman Hannah would have been able to describe to Chris, had she asked, for fear of her girlfriend noticing Hannah turning as red as Liesel's hair. When Hannah questioned Liesel about her time in the Tower, she was unable to remember how she had got up there in the first place. Following the visit, Hannah did some research and found out that Martha, previously high up in one of the big petrol companies, had been caught up in the same train bombing as Hannah's dad. Unlike him, she survived the attack, but it left her permanently paralysed below the waist.

When Hannah looks properly at the woman walking beside her, she knows why her dulled eyes are so familiar. In them, she sees her grandma, locked in an eternal battle with her brain, as she desperately tried to remember why the twins in front of her – Hannah and Fred – were calling her Nana.

How on earth are you going to write a 'think piece' good enough for Strickland, if all your interviewees have forgotten everything, Hannah asks herself.

And how have they forgotten?

? – she taps into her phone – *drugs?*

'She's still got one,' the woman says to the man, pointing to Hannah's mobile.

'You're right Megan, she does.'

'Don't show Benthe,' Megan says quietly, looking around.

'She says devices are divisive,' the man tells Hannah. She taps the phrase into her device – it would make a nice subheading. She isn't wrong, this Benthe. The paperwork she had to fill out to get a phone for the reluctant Chris and her nervous self. Not new models, of course. And the phone does make people look at Hannah funny – they know that in having it, she is under the thumb of the Hand.

Not necessarily a good thing, argued Chris, *to have all their information monitored by them.*

Not necessarily the worst thing, retorted Hannah, *to keep the wolf from the door.*

'Do you agree?' Hannah asks him.

He shrugs. 'She is taking us where we want to go. Whether I agree or not is irrelevant.'

'Especially since we don't have our phones anymore,' Megan adds.

'I haven't had one since I woke up in the Tower.'

For all Hannah knows, she could be in possession of one of their phones, procured following the exodus.

Hannah asks them to tell her more about their existence over the past few years. Their descriptions vary in floridity, but are very similar to things she's heard before, written before, and read before. Hannah is not the only journalist to have interviewed Dwellers and although independent newspapers may not exist anymore, rumour has it that an underground press has started up on the Highgate edge of the great lake of London. Evidently, people – the government included – are hungry for knowledge. And in cities like London, that can't be the only thing people are hungry for. Hannah's boss, famously hard-hitting journalist Strickland herself, wrote a great piece last week about the positive and negative effects – there were far more positives, of course – of the new Agricultural law: a blanket ban on industrialised animal farming.

Hannah asks the two Dwellers if it is okay to record them. They agree, but they eye her phone with suspicion. The know as well as Hannah does that they are being listened to.

Megan and Colin describe the grey rooms, a green, shake-like mixture they ate for two out of their three daily meals. They can't tell Hannah what they did all day. Their eyes are bright and their voices are low in their throats, almost a growl. Boatswain walks tightly to Hannah's side. They can remember something about mealtimes (or 'gruel times' as Colin calls them). They argue over which of the Scientists were more relaxed, and who were sticklers. Colin can tell Hannah something about the Greenhouses, where he worked. Megan can describe in vague detail the kitchens, where she worked.

'They had this herb,' she says. 'It looked like basil, but smelt like toothpaste.'

'Aye, she's right,' Colin nods.

'When did you meet Benthesikyme?' Hannah asks them. 'Was it in the Tower?'

They both shake their heads.

'Outside, definitely. It was a sunny day, and I was just wandering.'

'Aye, same.' Colin nods.

She encourages them to explain why they chose to follow Benthesikyme to the coast, especially with the threat of what might come to pass.

'I want to wash it all away,' Megan shrugs, looking at Colin for help, her hooded eyes watery and slow. 'I thought it had all been washed away already.'

'Aye,' Colin gives Megan a brief smile and Hannah can see that he is both kind and very, very tired. 'We want to start again. Or stop, properly.'

Stop properly, Hannah types.

'She wants to make it to Lindisfarne,' Colin adds. Hannah hasn't got the gumption to tell them that Holy Island is, as far as she's aware, nothing more than a rocky outcrop with a castle on top. Instead, she asks them if they have family, if they are here with anyone.

'It's a good question, pet,' Colin says, 'and one we were trying to answer when you appeared.'

'Are you all alone out here?' Megan's question is in earnest, but it still lands. Hannah takes a deep breath, surprised by the images of an angry Chris and a tearful Fred battling for space in her head. Boatswain licks her hand.

'No,' she forces a small smile. 'No. I have Boatswain, and I do have people – not parents – my father died in a terrorist attack on a train, in the first wave of eco-terrorism.'

Colin and Megan murmur sadly.

Hannah continues. 'My brother was in a Tower, with you lot. He might still be in there now.'

Give a little, Strickland always says, *to get something back.*

She tells them she misses him, a pathetic attempt at describing how she really feels (and she calls herself a wordsmith) and that she's worried too much time has passed since they were last together.

'A lot has passed me by too, since I decided to put my name on the Tower list,' Colin says sadly. Hannah asks him why he did it.

'I was scared that I would die down here.' The tone of his voice is leaden with finality, she feels like she can't press him further. And anyway, she asks herself, what's to press? Those who now represent the Tower, the people with the real power, told them all that the end was coming, and that the Towers were their only hope; and then they began the Life Lottery, inciting riots and violence in the streets.

When confronted with red-faced, jowly experts, who were Colin or Megan or even Fred, for that matter, to question that?

'I was curious,' Megan says, quietly.

'About what?' Hannah asks.

'The Towers. Life after the end.' Boatswain lets out a small whine. 'This isn't it, though.'

'Isn't what?' Hannah asks.

'The end,' Megan says. And they all agree.

The end is still to come, Hannah writes onto her notes.

Benthesikyme Styx certainly thinks so.

*

Hannah and Benthesikyme finally meet as they near Morpeth. Silently giving up the aim to reach Lindisfarne, the group have been heading gently east towards the coast.

'Look, there she is!' Colin's voice is loud enough to surprise a trotting Boatswain, whose greying eyebrows rise. Megan clutches a bony hand to her chest, and clasps the other to her mouth.

Benthesikyme Styx is a bright burst of colour but for her smooth, dark head. She is handing out small wrapped chocolates from the type of box people used to give as gifts.

'They're only five years out of date!' Hannah hears her laugh with the bunch of people ahead of them. 'I used to love the coconut ones! And just look at what they're called! We certainly hope to celebrate soon, don't we?'

No one would lose Benthesikyme in a crowd. She is so tall. She wears a long yellow raincoat with wide sleeves and her cheeks shine hotly from her sharp face.

Hannah takes the Milky Way Styx offers, and wonders whether she is wearing lipstick. Styx frowns at Hannah, who wants her to stop looking, but also to never stop looking. Boatswain licks his chops.

'You're not from the Tower.'

Hannah is struck dumb in Benthesikyme's presence. The wind lifts the leader's hood around her head, a sudden neon halo. She frowns at Benthesikyme.

'You are too fat to have been in a Tower,' Benthesikyme states.

'Cheers,' Hannah croaks, finally finding her voice.

'You know what I mean.'

'I…do I?'

'Who are you?' she asks again and her low voice travels straight to Hannah's gut.

'Benthesikyme Styx,' Hannah begins, because her brain is still thawing.

'No no, I'm Benthe Styx,' she says cautiously, seemingly ready to turn and run at any moment.

'Oh, oh, I know,' Hannah gulps, finally functioning again. 'I just wanted to make sure I was talking to–'

'Why?'

'I'm a journalist with Fresh Start. We're a partner magazine to the National Press.'

'You're from the NP?'

Hannah nods, fumbles in her coat pocket for card, but Styx keeps talking:

'Name?'

'Excuse me?'

'I said, what's your name?'

She shows the ID. She says, 'May. Hannah May.'

'Maaaaay, she will sta-ay-ay,' Benthe sings at her.

'Simon and Garfunkel. Yeah, I've had that one before. So anyway, my boss, Doctor Jaimini–'

'Strickland sent you?'

'Y-yes.'

'We're so glad to have you. Travel in peace.'

'Thank you.' And then, 'How do you know Strickland?'

'She has a reputation.' And then, 'What do you want with these people?'

'With your followers?'

'They're not followers.'

Hannah turns and asks her new companions, 'Megan, Colin, are you following Benthe?'

'Definitely,' says Megan, quietly.

'One hundred percent,' says Colin. Two other hooded figures in front of their group nod.

'Because you're our leader, Benthe,' Megan adds, looking at her feet as she says it.

Benthe Styx sighs. 'You don't need a leader; the Wave will make that clearer to you.'

Megan smiles tremulously as Benthe puts a hand, all long fingers and smooth skin, on her shoulder and squeezes. Then she turns to Hannah, all the softness in her voice completely gone. 'Shall we walk somewhere quieter?'

'If you have time.'

'I always have time for the big time,' she nods at Hannah. 'If people are interested in what we're doing here, and not just checking up on me.'

'I'm interested,' Hannah shrugs, unable to promise anything more. She feels herself leaning into Benthe's gaze.

Boatswain butts at Hannah's leg with his head. The three of them start walking.

*

'Your dog is very wise,' Benthe tells Hannah, as Boatswain pads in the middle, finding the painted lines of the motorway more comfortable to walk on than the tarmac. Or perhaps he is a canine barrier, protecting Hannah. Perhaps the two of them have spent too much time together, but Hannah's nose itches and her hair is on end as Benthe glides alongside. Hannah can't decide yet if she's scared of her, or if she… feels something else.

'He's my brother's dog, actually,' Hannah tells her. 'Fred. He went up into the Tower.'

Benthe nods. 'These are the things we lost when the world ended.'

Hannah asks her what she lost. Benthe tells her she gained a sense of self, a new purpose; an understanding that the only timetable she should have been following was the tides, that the only light she should look for was the moon. She had been scared when the river Tees began to take bits of her town away from her. She had wanted to be in a Tower, she tells Hannah, who taps diligently into her phone, wishing now she could have recorded Benthe's great long sentences. But then, Benthe explains, she saw that the moon was full, and was lighting her path.

Hannah tries desperately not to roll her eyes. Not at Benthe, but at herself because she doesn't want to roll her eyes at all. How can Hannah not want to roll her eyes at this woman? Chris would find her ridiculous. 'A sophisticated hippie with an obviously good education.'

'Did you make it to a Tower?'

'I was never in the Tower. I am a refugee.'

'A refugee?'

'Yes, the bastards tried to drown me, like a rat.' Her accent is southern, despite her backstory. Hannah almost smiles at her pronunciation of barrrstards.

'Tried?'

'They succeeded in drowning many of my loved ones, in ruining my home, but not my mind, nor my spirit.'

Even Boatswain whines at that one.

'Who are 'they' exactly? Who do you blame?'

'What don't I blame?'

'Erm…'

'Look, Miss May–'

'Ms.'

'What?'

'I prefer *Ms.*'

'Okay, fine, Ms May, what you need to know about me is right in front of you. I wear it all on my sleeve.' Her sleeves are attached to a bright orange and voluminous coat. A coat that would only help to drown you, in a flood.

Not all of it, Hannah thinks. 'So, do you think the wave will come?'

'I know it will. And soon. No more than a few days.'

'How do you know?'

'There is a tug in my thighs, nausea in my stomach.'

'Sounds like you're on your period.'

'Well, maybe we are about to be ejected from our safe womb.'

Hannah can't help it. She splutters with the ridiculousness of this shining, beautiful woman.

'Excuse me,' she apologises, 'but do you have any scientific basis to your... belief? If I am on a wild goose chase, the NP will not be pleased. Everyone reads us – even the top dogs in the Tower.'

Benthe growls. She reaches deep into a capacious sleeve and pulls out a smartphone. She looks around furtively.

'What's your email–'

'I cannot believe you have a phone! Megan and Colin said–'

'Email!'

'But the government Tower reads everything we send, are you su–'

'Ms May, just tell me your address.'

Hannah does as she's told. Benthe taps and clicks and her phone buzzes.

'Read it. We'll talk when we arrive.'

*

To: e.collinge@freshstartmag.np.uk

From: h.may@freshstartmag.np.uk

Subject: help

Emily, need you to cast an eye over this for me. I understand the data about the unprecedented sea level rise (up to thirty metres!), but am unsure about the last few pages. Specifically – how does what I am reading tell me a freak wave could occur and hit the coast of Northumberland in just a few days' time? No one on this job is telling me the whole truth.

Ta, Han

PS. Least you can do after telling Strickland that Chris left me.

*

The group reach Widdrington as night falls. Perhaps Benthe had been aiming for Druridge Bay... but the bay is gone.

131

Hannah can smell how close the sea is. The gutted, weather-torn cottages that were once homes glow with small fires – Dwellers, beachcombers, nature's residents. The grasses rustle with their whispers. It is cold and the sea is just a dark, chilly void. Boatswain, normally a huge fan of water, leans on her. She tells him he's a good boy. She feels her phone vibrate in her pocket.

It is the government-installed messaging app:

Han, I got your email. 21.20
It is big stuff!! 21.20
Where did you get it? 21.21
Msg back ASAP pls! 21.21
It looks like govt docs. 21.22
Or a very good imitation. 21.22

That explains why Emily's messages are getting through. Whatever is going on, they either already know about it or want to know more. Hannah frowns down at the green light in her hand.

What? 21.22
How do you know? 21.23
… (Emily is typing)

'Will you camp with us?'

Benthe at her shoulder makes Hannah almost wet herself in surprise. She nods dumbly, shrugs acceptingly.

'You have a sleeping bag,' Benthe smiles, 'but no tent, I see?'

'Strickland said she would send someone with–'

'I prefer the presumptuous look on you,' the divine leader grins. 'Don't ruin it by blaming it on your boss. She's a busy woman.'

Hannah feels her cheeks grow hot. She can barely see Benthe, but she knows she is smiling. Hannah has never thought of herself as presumptuous.

'Your dog doesn't like the dark? He is trembling.'

Hannah finds that she is too, but it isn't the cold or the dark. There is a pull on the limbs that are nearest to Benthe. She takes a deep breath.

'You feel it too, Ms May.'

'It?'

'The pull.'

Hannah says nothing, tries to catch her breath.

'Come,' Benthe takes her chilled fingers in a warm, silken hand. 'Let's eat.'

*

As a kid, with Fred, you adored camping. You and he would lie there while your dad snored, and you stared up into the never-quite-dark canvas, and whispered about all the monsters that were circling that safe pod. You always needed to pee and Fred would either scare you relentlessly with creepy sounds the whole time you squatted in a bush nearby or go with you to the toilet block, his hand on your shoulder to guide. Even now, when you think of your twin, you smell damp earth and hear the night chirping of crickets.

*

Benthe's tent is as bare as she is bright. There are two mats (now who is presumptuous?) and a torch dangles from the central pole.

'I don't want too much debris left when the Wave hits. When we are reborn, we don't want to spend time cleaning up the mess of the past.'

'Isn't that the meaning of life?' Hannah asks Benthe. The leader's laugh warms Hannah up. Boatswain, relieved to be lying down and to have received half a sandwich, sets up the barrage of farts he produces most nights to let Hannah know that he's relaxed.

'I'm sorry about him.' Hannah doesn't mean it. She is glad of his smelly heft at her feet.

Benthe's voice centres Hannah. The ocean sweeps and thunders just outside the tent. Everything they eat tastes pre-salted.

'You must have more questions,' she nudges Hannah's elbow.

Hannah asks her to talk about where she got the information about the wave.

'I have ways and means.'

Hannah wants to press her, but she is once again struck dumb. Everything is strange, yet Benthe is certain. *Yeah, and beautiful,* Hannah hears Chris scoff.

I haven't shared a bed with anyone but the dog since you left! Hannah snaps back, justifying her behaviour as she inches a little closer to Benthesikyme Styx.

*

Hannah wants to believe that there is nothing else going on, that Benthe is a true lunatic, and her reports are fabricated, and that the Dwellers who have followed are just gullible, as is proven by their entrance to the Towers in the first place – and their subsequent descent.

Hannah wants to check her phone, to read the email Emily has surely sent by now. She searches for it as best she can in the low tent, but can't put her hands on it and as she gropes around, she accidentally grabs Benthe's hand.

'Ms May!' Benthe giggles, and Hannah knows what she is doing with her voice and her slight movements towards her, but Hannah doesn't care. She wonders whether Strickland would be impressed or disappointed if something happened between them, especially if Hannah isn't allowed to put it on the record.

Nose to nose, Benthe whispers, 'The people you've come to find—'

'The people I have come to find?'

133

'Your brother... and someone else, maybe?'

'H-how did you... but I'm not really looking for them – for him.'

'I don't believe you,' Benthe tells Hannah, and Hannah feels her breath against her cheek. Hannah has nothing she can say to that.

'You need to let them leave your mind.' Benthe is so quiet, Hannah has to strain to hear her above the call of the North Sea. 'If you don't, the Wave won't be able to clean you. You won't make it.' Benthe shuffles right up to Hannah, 'I want you to make it.'

*

Of course, she's gone when Hannah wakes up. Boatswain is pawing at the tent, desperate to be let out. She opens the flap into a bright white day. Remembering again where he is, Boatswain legs it straight on to the muddy patch of grass before them.

That's when Hannah sees it.

Her phone, half buried in the mud, just outside the tent. She pulls it out. Wipes it on her trousers. It is scratched and damp, but it still works.

One hundred and five missed messages from Emily. Countless missed phone calls from Strickland. And at last, a message from Chris.

She puts her phone to her ear. She is going to put her career first, of course, as Chris always complains that she does, but she can't bear to read the message from Chris yet, she'll feel too guilty. She watches as Boatswain tries to eat some seaweed.

That's when she sees it.

The water.

It is still. Dark. Quiet.

Too quiet.

Then Boatswain feels it too. Something is wrong.

His tail sneaks between his legs. He backs up the bank, whining softly. Hannah hears Strickland's panicked warnings in her ear:

Hannah, turn around. Get to higher ground. Styx obviously isn't just a lunatic, she knows what she is talking about and it is coming, Hannah, the Wave. Get out, Hannah. Get. Out.

Hannah can see nothing on the horizon but a line of grey-green. It looks still, but as she stares, it starts to bleed into heavy clouds, like smudges at the edge of a painting.

Hannah looks for the message from Chris. She doesn't know what else to do.

Han, I'm sorry I didn't tell you where I was going. I've been up north visiting family.

How many people have been lying to Hannah today? Chris has no family 'up north'. What has she been doing?

Took the tent (I hope you didn't need it). Have found some transport at an abandoned checkpoint on the Border, so am coming home now. Not far from what used to be Druridge Bay. Trying to avoid the Dwellers (there seem to be loads up here!) Anyways, I'll be home in an hour or so. I love you (and Boaty, of course) x x

The dog pants up at Hannah, eyes white in his head.

The mud in front of them begins to glisten slightly.

Without thinking, Hannah hits dial. The call goes to voicemail.

'Chris. Come find me. I'm with the Dwellers. Widdrington. Hurry.'

The thought enters Hannah's head that if anyone survives this, someone one day might write a piece all about the stupid journalist who was duped by a gorgeous–

'Ms May.'

Benthe is standing in front of her. The wave in the distance gives her the appearance of having aqua-marine wings.

'Look who I found,' she says and pulls into Hannah's line of vision a man, close to middle-age, slightly balding, but with tufts of yellow-blond hair, the same shade as hers; and now the dog is howling and yelping and jumping all over him and Hannah's heart feels like cold liquid, like the sea itself sloshing about inside her, and her thighs feel a drag, a pull, as she kneels in the wet dirt and gestures for Fred, her brother, her twin, her childhood hero to come to her, please, because she just can't move anymore, she just can't.

*

To: h.may@freshstartmag.np.uk
From: j.strickland@freshstartmag.np.uk
Subject: Re: Think Piece
Hannah,
Is this all true? Chris rescuing you in a stolen army van? The unnerving quiet of the ocean? The disappeared sand dunes?

According to the updates from the Tower, the Wave made landfall an hour ago. You have just woken up for the third time, imagining you are still in the tent. With Benthe.

You know the rules on theft, not to mention sensationalism, we won't get published. It could be an offence! Promise me it is true. Because if it is... wow! If the van was empty and abandoned... Chris might just get away with it.

Your hand still hurts from where you gripped Fred's, lying on the flat-bed of the truck, just like the good old camping days except now the two of you couldn't look behind you, for fear of an advancing wall of water. Your brain is full of the faces you met on the way to the coast, of Megan and Colin and dazzling Benthe, the lovely lunatic, who is paying for her self-belief.

Of course, it is going to be difficult to publish straight away – what with the loss of life – but I'm forwarding you half your pay now. All above board (and water!)

Chris groans beside you, the bright light of the phone making her eyelids flicker. In the living room, Fred snores on the sofa. You roll over, blocking the light with your body. You don't want to have another argument about her concealed life. You suspect she is a terrorist. She suspects you are unfaithful.

You scroll down.

I'd like to know a bit more about Styx herself – the person behind the legacy (or martyr... is she a martyr now?) – but I suppose with everything going on – the lines about you finding your brother are almost poetic–

Strickland is artful with the *almost*-compliment.

– that you didn't have time to get to know her better. Still, if there is anything else you could include about her, I'd be grateful –

–Chris wouldn't... but then, she's been lying too.

– either way, it is good writing –

Strickland, you've done it again –

– I've marked up the things I would change.

What a relief, it was all seeming too good to be true!

Best,
J. Strickland

*

After that first Wave, there is another one, and another. All those Dwellers who thought it was safe to return... how many were lost?

You refuse to go to the coast ever again. You read a government paper about what happens to a person's body under the weight of several tons of water and you lie awake at night, with tears pooling in your ears. Eventually, you unpack the bag you took with you on the trip. At the bottom, you find a crumpled piece of paper, scrawled with the handwriting of someone no longer alive:

Congratulations, Ms May – you survived the Wave!
Welcome to the New World.
Love, B

After

2042

Generation B

'I thought we had a meeting now, what are you doing? Lin? Lin?' Helen is banging on the bathroom door.

Lin isn't my name, but Helen says she refuses to call me by a number. She says that I must have been given a name, since I was born on the outside. When she says that, my lips in muscle-memory form around the letter 'Z', but it gets no further.

Helen claims that it is her moral duty as a woman to give other young women names and therefore, voices. She has some weird ideas, but that's why I'm here, as her Mentor. To sort them out for her.

'You okay?'

'Helen…' I start to growl at her. Her name still sounds so strange in my mouth. She says that when she was young, it was a perfectly normal, quite boring name. She tells me that when I pronounce it in my way, it makes her feel old.

'Sorry, I meant are you all right?' Helen amends her language.

'Well…' I look down at the blood on my pants. It is dark and not like the sort of stuff that comes out of the cuts I sometimes get on my hands when I am working in the Greenhouse and forget my gloves.

'Lin?' She knocks on the door.

'You can come in,' I shrug.

'What is–' her face, flushed from climbing up to my sector, tells me that she didn't expect for me to still be sitting on the toilet. Nakedness in general used to be frowned upon in the old-world, when people like Helen and, I guess, my parents, lived Outside. She struggles to say anything, just turns around so that my face is facing her bottom. Not that she really has one, the material of her blue overalls falls straight down from her shoulders. The cubicle isn't really big enough for two.

'I'd rather see your face,' I tell her, and she slowly turns, looking very hard at my eyes.

'Why am I in here, Lin?'

Helen is always exasperated with me.

*

There is blood in my knickers. I lean my forehead against the cubicle wall and let it sink in. Acceptance that my life can continue as normal. Happiness that nothing needs to change. Sweet relief! Before I get my hands dirty, I pull my phone from my coat pocket and text him: Drink later?

*

Helen's face is one big grin.

'Finally, I get to teach you something,' she says, and her goading voice is not attractive on someone so old. I tell her this and she stops smiling. Then she looks at my pants again and frowns.

'It is just like with our Jane!' Helen's eyes are a little misty. I frown.

'Jane?' I say, uncertainly.

'I had a sister, once. Lost her though. She lived in Spain, and when everything fell apart, we never could get in touch.'

I am silent, still sitting on the toilet. My bum is getting numb. I do not need Helen to take a trip down memory lane right now.

'Do you know what this is?' She waves her hand in the direction of the blood. Frustrated, I shake my head. 'That is why I called you in here, Helen.' I say her name wrong on purpose and she exhales loudly. She looks around the tiny space, knocks here and there on the walls.

'What are you doing?' I am bored of sitting now. My legs are fizzing and popping. She continues to press, to run her thumbnail along certain parts of the wall.

'Looking…for,' she knocks just under the sink, then shrugs to herself, 'a cupboard or…' She sticks her head into the round plastic shower container, 'somewhere you store stuff…'

'Stuff?

'I don't know – pads or tampons or sanitary towels or–'

'I sent my towel to the laundry this morning–'

'No, sanitary towels, things that you use to keep the blood from ruining your knickers.'

My skin chills. I can't tell which is colder – my feet or the floor. I look up at Helen, unable to speak. Her face, which is normally taut with disappointment, softens. She blinks a few times.

*

I wake up to blood. I know what I'm going to find, so I put off going to the toilet for as long as I can. I lie in the grey of the early morning. The dog watches me watch the ceiling, but she's still too tired to bother me for breakfast. My full bladder and the pains make me nauseous, but still, I wait until I absolutely can't hold it any longer. What am I waiting for anyway? There is nothing there to hold onto.

*

I clean myself off with a jet of water. Helen gives me a flannel to fold into my pants.

'I feel ridiculous,' I tell her, through the door, trying to work out how not to waddle. I hear Helen laugh slightly.

When I come out of the bathroom, she's poured us both a glass of water and is sitting in the chair under the window. I sit down on my bed and peer up into the grey light.

'It should be a cup of tea with three sugars,' she nods at me as I take a sip of water. 'That's what my mum gave me and Jane, when we had our first.'

'Your first what?' My thighs ache. All I want to do is sleep. What is happening?

'Period,' Helen says quietly. She pushes her short black hair from her face. 'You're menstruating.'

*

When I first saw the blood, I thought I was dying. I screamed the supermarket toilet down, forgetting my eleven-year-old self and bawling my eyes out. Dad thought someone was bothering me and burst into the ladies' loo, fists drawn. I think he'd have preferred a fight with a weirdo in the women's toilets over what he actually had to deal with.

*

I had read about menstruation. We had been sent an article to read in study time. I shut my eyes, try to remember. It can't be possible, can it? I see words pop behind my forehead – words like egg and tube and womb and fertile.

I look at my pupil. She looks back at me, her light eyes disappearing under the small shaft of sunlight poking through the cloud.

What else did the article say?

That the 'mens' bit of the word related to the word for 'month' in the old Romance languages. Oh no. Every month? I look at Helen. As if reading my mind, she nods.

That it could last around forty years of a *woman's* life.

'So, I'm a woman? In the old-world sense?' I ask Helen, who is very well equipped to answer since she is an old-world woman. And strangely proud of it. She tells me off if I write up our weekly minutes and refer to her as 'they'. She says she likes her gendered pronouns, her *she*s and her *her*s. Says they make her think of home and her sister and her mum (mother) and a cat she once had, who she'd called Princess. A strange feminine name that made Helen smile as she said it and then, straight after, cry.

The Scientists task Mentors like me with the endeavour of removing what they call this type of 'pride hangover' from the old-worlders we look after, but Helen's attitude toward her 'gender' has never weakened, no matter how hard I have tried to prove to her that the lack of labelling has created the fairer society we now live in.

But now – *well, shit,* as Helen would say. Now I've gone and been labelled by her, marked by this blood currently soaking into… what did Helen call it? A sanitary towel? Nothing about this strikes me as sanitary.

*

Hide it. Hide it, clean it, put mud on your legs so that it looks like you've just been playing in the dirt with your cousin. Hide it. Don't let him see it. He'll say you're ready, he'll wheel you out like he did your sister, and you know how that ended. A crying orphan with your sister's dancing eyes.

*

Helen has become a human question machine.

Helen: 'Do you know of anyone else in your Mentor group who's had their (well, *her*, actually) period?'

Helen: 'Has anyone ever discussed any protocols with you about this?'

Helen: 'How do you feel?'

Helen: 'Does your stomach hurt?'

Helen: 'And your legs? Is there like a... dragging feeling?'

Helen: 'Are you crying?'

Helen: 'Lin?'

*

Victory! I'm bleeding! Ha! And you thought you'd shut down, body. You thought the thick hair on the backs of my legs and the bald spot on the back of my head were all I had left! Ha! Now my longed-for thigh-gap bears the traces of my internal functions. Even as my stomach clenches and the small of my back aches, I promise that I will never complain about my period again.

*

'I used to crave ham the week before my period,' Helen tells me, when I have quietened down. She has moved onto the bed and is stroking my head, which I have in her lap. Her fingers are coolly welcome on my scalp. She smells friendly, all warm fabric and warm human.

'What's ham?' I am exhausted by all the new knowledge. I have just discovered that I can menstruate. Perhaps the only one who can on my storey. Perhaps the only one in my Generation. I think of the faces of my fellow Generation B-ers and I wonder which of them would be old-world 'women'.

Who do I think I am, to categorise the faces of my friends?

'A flattened and sliced, delicious attempt at using up all the last scraps of pork.'

'Pork?'

'Pig-meat.'

'Pigs...' I think for a moment. 'Are they those pink farm animals from the old-world?'

Helen nods. 'They used to make this oink sound.'

'What was that?' I turn onto my back to look at her. I can see right up her nostrils as she snorts heavily, pretending to be a 'pig'. I can't help but laugh. In the ensuing silence in the room, we hear the call to dinner for our floor.

143

'Are you hungry?' Helen asks, looking towards the door. 'These meetings normally make you so hangry.'

'Hangry?' Again, I am confused.

'Hungry and angry.' She pokes me softly in one aching side. My skin becomes a layer of standing hairs. I flush at her attention.

Is this what it feels like to have a parent?

I wouldn't know – they told me that my parents left me here, during the Exodus, over a decade ago. A Scientist who remembers them said that they had promised me that they would come back. That they were the ones who helped design the Tower, our home – but they didn't come back.

They left the Tower a day before the first lot of Waves.

I am quite glad for Helen.

It is a strange day and so I am having strange thoughts.

*

A spoonful of honey to make your future periods easier. A cake to celebrate. Red wine to put the blood back in your cheeks. A special meal and balloons to see if your father asks why we're celebrating. A party for the whole town, so everyone knows!

*

I decide I don't want to go to dinner. Let the Scientists come and check on us. I'll show them my pants. That'll quiet them down.

'You'll have to tell them when you're ready.'

'Why?' I feel fractious. I sit up and back away from her, leaning against the wall. 'I don't want anyone to know.'

Helen laughs in the same way that she does when she thinks she's won a debate. It is a self-satisfied laugh that makes her look ancient. I stare at her, furious. She sees my face and starts to laugh harder.

'What is it? Why are you laughing?'

'Because you're ashamed of your period. Even though half an hour ago you didn't know what it was! How is it possible that the patriarchy has managed to survive the apocalypse that it pretty much – let's be honest here – created? That is has travelled all the way up here to make you embarrassed of your functioning, working body?'

I gasp. Helen has never said such taboo words in my presence before. I take her in through wide eyes.

'Don't say the A word, remember.' My voice is too quiet to carry the Mentor-authority the Scientists trained us in. 'Or the P one.'

Helen rolls her eyes, shrugs. 'Have it your way, Lin.'

See? See how Helen is always frustrated with me?

*

In the house where I grew up, we had a chiming clock. Complete with a pendulum

144

and everything. It would gong its way through the hours. If I woke in the middle of the night, I would wait for the comfort of its next set of chimes, safe in the knowledge that I was only ever fifteen minutes away from the next sound.

Sometimes, I still hear imaginary chimes. I check and, without fail, the clock on the kitchen wall assures me that wherever that old time-teller is now, it is still correctly singing.

It is like that with my period. Even now, mid-way through the occasional month, I feel a familiar twist in my stomach, an ache in my groin. I expect a sudden rush of warmth as I stand up. My body remembers.

*

She checks on me, before her night-shift. She is on duty in the sick rooms. Her face has gone all floppy and kind again. I take it as an apology. I've mentored her long enough to know that I'll not get a verbal one. I am in bed with a reading-screen, having borrowed that damned article from the study-room. She sits in the chair, looks at me with her head inclined.

'I'll see what supplies I can find, so you don't have to keep rinsing your towel,' she sighs, after staring at me for a moment.

I nod. 'Thank you.'

'If you have stomach pains, hold something warm against it. Even your hand will do.'

I act as if I am reading. I nod. 'Will do.'

'Any more questions, before I go?' She asks, a slight smile on her face. This is my line, normally. I growl. She laughs, her eyebrows shooting up.

'No.'

She shrugs, stands up, smooths down her overalls.

'Don't get angry…' she starts, and I narrow my eyes at her. 'I did a bit of bartering and got you this.' She removes something from her front pocket. 'Don't worry, I got it from contraband so long ago, everyone has forgotten it,' her voice sounds as if it is coming from a different room. 'It used to work a treat when I was your age. Call it an 'old-world' remedy.'

A shining purple package lands hefty at my feet. I can just make out three silvered letters. A 'c' an 'h' and an 'o'.

Message Deleted

Welcome to Tower 3's Internal System (T3IS)! Please type your issue in the box below and one of our Helpers will respond as quickly as possible. We apologise for any delay in response time, we are experiencing a high frequency of queries. 07:15

GenA/1012/Blue: I am trapped in my room. 07:16

H24: Hello, I am Helper24. How can I help? 07:18

GenA/1012/Blue: I am trapped in my room. 07:18

H24: I see that you think you are trapped in your room. 07:18

GenA/1012/Blue: I don't think I am. I know I am. My door won't open. 07:19
GenA/1012/Blue: Room 212. 07:19

H24: Just to make sure we are in contact with the real you, we need to ask you some security questions. 07:19

GenA/1012/Blue: The real me? I've been here too long to remember the real me. 07:19

H24: *message deleted* 07:20
H24: First question: What is your generation code? 07:20

GenA/1012/Blue: A. The first. I was there at the end. 07:20
GenA/1012/Blue: The start. And I remember everything, Helper24, so tell them the drugs aren't working. 07:20

H24: So, Gen. A 07:22

GenA/1012/Blue: Yes. 07:22

H24: Awesome! Can I just remind you that these conversations are recorded for security and training purposes? 07:23

GenA/1012/Blue: Sure. 07:23

H24: Great! Just a couple more questions before I can access your keypad and see what the issue is. 07:25

GenA/1012/Blue: The issue is that I am trapped in my room. 07:25

H24: Absolutely. Second question. What is your sector? 07:25

GenA/1012/Blue: Blue. 07:25
GenA/1012/Blue: doesn't my username tell you all this? 07:26
GenA/1012/Blue: Hello? It is Blue. Blue, Room 212. 07:27

H24: Good, okay. Final question. What is your room number? 07:28

GenA/1012/Blue: Really? 07:28
GenA/1012/Blue: Fine. My room number is 212. 07:30

H24: Fantastic! I've found you. Nice to meet you, number 1012. 07:30

GenA/1012/Blue: And you, Helper24. 07:30

H24: Oh, you can call me 24. 07:31
H24: *message deleted* 07:31

GenA/1012/Blue: Are you flirting with me, 24? 07:31

H24: *message deleted* 07:31
H24: So, 1012, how can I help you today? 07:32

GenA/1012/Blue: I am trapped in my room. The door won't open. 07:32
GenA/1012/Blue: The keypad lights are off. 07:33

H24: Have you tried the keypad? 07:33

GenA/1012/Blue: The lights are off. 07:34

H24: This happens sometimes 1012. Would it be okay for us to go through the potential causes in order to find the correct solution? 07:35

GenA/1012/Blue: *message deleted* 07:35
GenA/1012/Blue: If it gets me out of my room, yes. 07:35

H24: Perfect. 07:35
H24: Question 1 07:35
H24: What have you done in your quarters since lockdown last night? 07:36

GenA/1012/Blue: Lockdown?? 07:36

H24: Excuse me, I meant after curfew. 07:37

GenA/1012/Blue: They lock the doors on us? 07:37

H24: *message deleted* 07:40
H24: *message deleted* 07:40
H24: it is for your safety :) 07:40

GenA/1012/Blue: ??? 07:41
GenA/1012/Blue: I am still trapped in here. 07:41
GenA/1012/Blue: Hello? 24? 07:41

H24: I apologise for the delay. 07:45
H24: Please tell us about your movements after yesterday's curfew. 07:45

GenA/1012/Blue: I had a shower. 07:46

H24: Was it your only shower of the day? 07:46

GenA/1012/Blue: Seriously? Yes. Yes, it was. 07:46
GenA/1012/Blue: I follow the rules when they make sense. 07:46

H24: And when they don't make sense? 07:47

GenA/1012/Blue: *message deleted* 07:47
GenA/1012/Blue: After my shower, I read. 07:47

H24: Until what time? 07:48

GenA/1012/Blue: Lights off. 07:48

H24: What are you reading, 1012? 07:48

GenA/1012/Blue: *message deleted* 07:48
GenA/1012/Blue: Does this make a difference to my keypad? 07:48

H24: No. 07:49
H24: I'm just interested. 07:49
H24: Sorry. 07:49

GenA/1012/Blue: Oh, right. 07:50
GenA/1012/Blue: I've taken two books out from the library. 07:50
GenA/1012/Blue: Things I never had time to read in the past. 07:50
GenA/1012/Blue: Russian classics. A collection of short stories, a novel. 07:50
GenA/1012/Blue: Lots of twists, some romance. 07:50

H24: I'm a science-fiction fan myself. Used to love that *Gaia* series. We don't stock that, up here. 07:51

GenA/1012/Blue: You must love all this then. 07:51

H24: I thought I would. 07:51
H24: *message deleted* 07:51

GenA/1012/Blue: 24? You still there? 07:53

H24: I am, 1012. 07:55
H24: Last night/this morning, did you touch any of the light fixtures in your room? 07:56

GenA/1012/Blue: No. 07:56
GenA/1012/Blue: You switch it all off centrally, don't you? 07:56

H24: I have as much control over the lights as you do, 1012. 07:57

GenA/1012/Blue: Awful, isn't it? 07:57

H24: *message deleted* 07:58
H24: That eliminates any issues with the circuitry. 07:59
H24: Please bear with me while I update your account. 07:59

GenA/1012/Blue: I have an account? 07:59
GenA/1012/Blue: Of course I do. 07:59
GenA/1012/Blue: Why am I surprised? 07:59

H24: Thank you for your patience. 08:03
H24: I have an account too. 08:03
H24: Everyone in the Tower has one. 08:04

GenA/1012/Blue: Even the top dogs? 08:04

H24: Even them. 08:05
H24: Woof woof. 08:05

GenA/1012/Blue: Ha! 08:05
GenA/1012/Blue: *message deleted* 08:06

H24: Great, I have updated your account. 08:07

GenA/1012/Blue: I am so relieved. 08:07

H24: Okay, next series of questions: what is your job? 08:08

GenA/1012/Blue: Doesn't my account tell you this? 08:07
GenA/1012/Blue: Hello? 08:08
GenA/1012/Blue: I am currently unemployed. 08:08

H24: Please choose the reason for your unemployment from the options below
(you can choose more than one):
a)   above working age (Generation A)
b)   below working age (Generation B)
c)   unsuited to prior career path
d)   suffering from mental health issues
e)   suffering from physical health issues
f)   other   08:08

GenA/1012/Blue: f) other 08:09

H24: Please explain your choice further. 08:09

GenA/1012/Blue: 24, you're so nosy! 08:10

GenA/1012/Blue: How do I know you're authorised to ask me these questions? 08:10

H24: *message deleted* 08:11
H24: my badge number is: 290717. 08:11
H24: Please type it into the search bar to check my authorisation. 08:11

GenA/1012/Blue: No need to get snotty with me, 24. I thought we were friends. 08:12
GenA/1012/Blue: 24, are you still there? 08:13
GenA/1012/Blue: I'm going to miss breakfast at this rate. 08:15
GenA/1012/Blue: Or maybe I shouldn't call it breakfast. That's a bit 'old-world' … 08:16
GenA/1012/Blue: Sustenance. I am going to miss sustenance at this rate. 08:16

H24: Please explain why you have chosen option f. 08:20

GenA/1012/Blue: Oh, you're back! It must have been really urgent… 08:20
GenA/1012/Blue: I mean, I'm actually trapped in here… 08:20
GenA/1012/Blue: Fine! 08:20
GenA/1012/Blue: I am on trial. 08:20

H24: *message deleted* 08:21
H24: again? 08:21

GenA/1012/Blue: What?? 08:21

H24: what did you do? 08:21

GenA/1012/Blue: *message deleted* 08:22
GenA/1012/Blue: is this a badge question, 24? 08:22

H24: no. 08:22

GenA/1012/Blue: if I have to be serious, you have to be serious. 08:22
GenA/1012/Blue: Read my account. 08:23
GenA/1012/Blue: It will tell you what you need to know. 08:23

H24: I do not have that level of authorisation. 08:24

GenA/1012/Blue: Oh dear. 08:24

GenA/1012/Blue: Woof woof 08:24

H24: Indeed. 08:24
GenA/1012/Blue: They don't think I hurt anyone. 08:25
GenA/1012/Blue: You're not speaking to a new-world murderer or anything. 08:25

H24: … 08:26

GenA/1012/Blue: If we discuss what I am accused of, will you promise to open the door? 08:26
GenA/1012/Blue: Hello? 08:26
GenA/1012/Blue: 24? 08:26

H24: I promise. 08:26

GenA/1012/Blue: Right. 08:27
GenA/1012/Blue: Okay. 08:27
GenA/1012/Blue: *message deleted* 08:27

H24: ?? 08:27

GenA/1012/Blue: They're accusing me of bringing in contraband 08:30
GenA/1012/Blue: Years ago. Before the Wave. 08:30
GenA/1012/Blue: At least, that's what they tell me. 08:30

H24: Wow! 08:30
H24: How? 08:30

GenA/1012/Blue: I don't know, because I didn't do it 08:31

H2: You're lying, 1012. 08:31

GenA/1012/Blue: What? 08:31
GenA/1012/Blue: *message deleted* 08:31
GenA/1012/Blue: Why would you say that? 08:32

H24: No one is ever accused without evidence. 08:32
H24: And there is your criminal record, from Before. 08:32
H24: Poison seeds, remember? 08:32

GenA/1012/Blue: How do you know about that? 08:32
GenA/1012/Blue: I was acquitted 08:32
GenA/1012/Blue: And anyway, what about innocent until proven guilty? 08:32

H24: Very original. Get that from one of your novels? 08:33
H24: Are you going to tell me the truth? 08:33

GenA/1012/Blue: Are you going to let me out? 08:34

H24: Depends what you had brought in. 08:34

GenA/1012/Blue: Seriously? 08:34
GenA/1012/Blue: H24? 08:34
GenA/1012/Blue: Fine! 08:35
GenA/1012/Blue: They say that I brought in condoms. 08:35
GenA/1012/Blue: and other types of contraception. 08:35

H24: Oh! 08:35
H24: *message deleted* 08:35

GenA/1012/Blue: Yup. 08:36

H24: I mean, contraband is bad but contraception… wow. 08:36

GenA/1012/Blue: Yup. 08:37
GenA/1012/Blue: It is a dangerous accusation to throw at someone. 08:37

H24: Especially someone like you, 1012. 08:37

GenA/1012/Blue: Like me? 08:38

H24: An ex-criminal. Someone who follows the rules 08:39
H24: When they make sense. 08:39

GenA/1012/Blue: *message deleted* 08:40
GenA/1012/Blue: are you going to let me out? 08:42

H24: Did you mean to poison that actor, in her own garden? 08:43

GenA/1012/Blue: *message deleted* 08:43

GenA/1012/Blue: No. 08:43

GenA/1012/Blue: Are you going to let me out? 08:43

H24: What do you think about the Contraception Amendment to our mission statement? 08:43

GenA/1012/Blue: which one is that? 08:44

H24: Click the link here if you'd like to read more. 08:45

GenA/1012/Blue: I was teasing. 08:45

GenA/1012/Blue: I know which one it is. 08:45

GenA/1012/Blue: They've already made me read it, thanks. 08:45

H24: Great, so you're aware that the use of any form of contraception contravenes quite a big rule? 08:45

GenA/1012/Blue: *message deleted* 08:46

GenA/1012/Blue: I am aware that you're all concerned about where your next lot of workers are going to come from, yes. 08:46

GenA/1012/Blue: sorry, I'm hungry. I didn't mean to use the 'w' word. 08:46

H24: That's okay. You're right, how we procure our generation C is important to us. 08:47

H24: It should be important to you too. 08:47

GenA/1012/Blue: Procure??? 08:48

GenA/1012/Blue: Can you let me out of my room now? 08:48

GenA/1012/Blue: Bit fed up of all the 'helpsplaining'. 08:48

H24: What did you barter for? 08:49

GenA/1012/Blue: I'm not guilty of contraband. 08:49

H24: There is quite an incriminating video on your account that says otherwise. 08:50

GenA/1012/Blue: *message deleted* 08:50

GenA/1012/Blue: now you tell me. 08:50

H24: So, what did you barter for? 08:51

GenA/1012/Blue: you know you're not letting me out of my room, right? 08:52
GenA/1012/Blue: I'm literally bartering for my 'freedom' 08:52

H24: The irony is not lost on me, 1012. 08:53
H24: So... 08:53
H24: ...what did you barter for? 08:53

GenA/1012/Blue: They were for personal use. 08:53

H24: Your account tells me you were well within your fifth decade when you joined us. 08:54

GenA/1012/Blue: *message deleted* 08:54
GenA/1012/Blue: So? 08:54

H24: So... we have come to understand that females in their sixth decade (which you now are) have little need for contraception. 08:54

GenA/1012/Blue: Ageist much? 08:55
GenA/1012/Blue: Heteronormative much? 08:55
GenA/1012/Blue: I thought this was the NEW WORLD 08:55
GenA/1012/Blue: I might still be menstruating! 08:57

H24: We have found that a loss of menstruation is a common side effect of living at such altitude. 08:58

GenA/1012/Blue: Have you now? 08:59

H24: Also, your account tells us your last period was three years before you arrived here. June, 2020. 09:00

GenA/1012/Blue: You know it all, don't you? 09:00

H24: Not everything, no. 09:00

GenA/1012/Blue: *message deleted* 09:01
GenA/1012/Blue: Who are you, 24? 09:01

H24: Helper 24, at your service. 09:01

GenA/1012/Blue: *message deleted* 09:01
GenA/1012/Blue: What about sexually transmitted infections, diseases? 09:02

H24: Every new arrival goes through rigorous testing. 09:02

GenA/1012/Blue: Indeed. 09:03

H24: Are you going to tell me the truth? 09:03

GenA/1012/Blue: My door is still locked. 09:04
GenA/1012/Blue: Hello? 09:04
GenA/1012/Blue: Fine. 09:04
GenA/1012/Blue: For chocolate. For wine. 09:04

H24: Red? White? 09:05

GenA/1012/Blue: So, you're a connoisseur now? 09:05
GenA/1012/Blue: Red. 09:05
GenA/1012/Blue: Cabernet. 09:05

H24: I was always partial to a single malt 09:06
H24: Gin was good too. 09:06

GenA/1012/Blue: Cheers to that. 09:07
GenA/1012/Blue: Can you let me out now? I need my gruel. 09:07
GenA/1012/Blue: 24? 09:07

H24: I'm afraid not. 09:08

GenA/1012/Blue: What? 09:08

H24: As I said at the very start of our conversation today, we are being monitored for security and training purposes. 09:08

GenA/1012/Blue: Okay. 09:09
GenA/1012/Blue: So, what? 09:10

H24: So, I am training to be part of Tower 3's Justice Team. 09:10

GenA/1012/Blue: *message deleted.* 09:10

H24: Thank you for your confession, 1012. 09:11
H24: Is there anything else I can help you with today? 09:11
GenA/1012/Blue: When will they come for me? 09:12

H24: I've already sent the alert. 09:12

GenA/1012/Blue: *message deleted*. 09:13

H24: Is there anything else I can help you with today? 09:14

GenA/1012/Blue: Will they be gentle? 09:14

H24: I have asked them to be, 1012. 09:14

GenA/1012/Blue: Will they listen to you? 09:15
GenA/1012/Blue: 24? 09:15

H24: Woof. 09:16

GenA/1012/Blue: *message deleted* 09:16

H24: Is there anything else I can help you with today? 09:18
H24: Is there anything else I can help you with today? 09:20
H24: I am going to terminate the chat now. Please reconnect if you have further questions.
I am Helper24 and I have been your Helper today. When I end this chat, a window will open asking if you would be happy to take a short survey about our service today. If you are happy to take the survey, please click the Yes, Survey Me! *button. From all of us here at T3IS – have a good day!* 09:22

A Valid Endeavour

You've been there, at the window, for most of the morning. If I get up close to take a look at you, you'll hide your face, move away, but your nearest eye has followed me around my quarters, slowly rotating in your sharp little skull.

Your stern appraisal of my tiny little space is breaking my heart. No, I don't have the sky. No, I can't feel the air on my face. I can imagine, rather than hear, the wind hurrying past. It does nothing to lift the hair that is beginning to grow back on my recently shorn head.

Not long before they shear me again.

I didn't realise birds could fly up this high, to the last floor of the blue sector. No more windows after this one! I assumed that if you tried, your head would explode. As it is, your beak does look more snubbed than I would expect for a gull. As if you were bred pressed right against the side of a box. And it's meant to be orange, isn't it? Your beak? Not the sort of greying pink that I can see occasionally tapping on the thick glass of my port-hole.

Your slight body takes up most of the light. In the gloom that is left, your feather-shadows ruffle on the wall above my bed. It is hypnotising to watch – my eyes blur, and I stare at the dark imprint of your moving shape, as I slump forward on my chair. It is a position my body finds familiar, yet one at which my mind shrugs with surprise. Today is gloomy enough for me to reach for the light switch. An old tic and, of course, futile. They don't put the power on in the daytime. Although... I do wonder if turning everything off from a main switchboard just to turn it back on again in seven hours is energy efficient. I don't really need to see, anyway. Conjuring the half-remembered sound of your unsubtle coos and the crackle of the wind in the nibs of your feathers is enough for me right now.

I'd like to keep you as a pet, if you would allow it. I could give you a name and a little collar and these actions would ground me, would stop this feeling that my very essence is escaping my body through unseen punctures, but of course, these actions would ground you, too. You're full of character. I could do with some of that energy. Being locked in here makes me feel as though somewhere just outside the door, the teenagers at the funeral are all getting pissed and smoking cigarettes.

Not in here. In here we are mourning seriously.

No one has visited me properly in days. The only contact I've had has been food delivery.

I want to celebrate the shock of black in the white of your wings. The ruler straight line of grey that adorns your back and head, your delicate pink feet and your cruel, misshapen beak.

You're beautiful, and primeval. I must write you down, that way I can keep you with me.

You must come from somewhere – most people here do. On meeting days – when I used to be permitted to go – people told you proudly about their soil, their lakes and forests. They preened about the height of their mountains, the mass of their cities. Their chests puffed with it all until, as the years pass, they begin to forget their heritage.

I wrote down where I was from, in case it slid from my head. It is on a note somewhere here. I know that I used to spend a lot of time in gardens. And I remember that my land was covered in cow parsley.

There are papers piled high by my pillow. Lists. Accounts. Memos – to remind myself of the things that I miss, before I forget to miss them. Maybe it is the altitude, or the mist, but my brain goes to mush up here. It feels grey and spongy when I shake my head. Everything is rationed and I am running out of people whom I recognise well enough to ask if I can borrow a pen, or more paper. It has been recycled so often that it is almost transparent anyway. I feel the same. When I hold my hand up to the scant light, my skin has the pallid glow of an energy saving bulb.

Still, I try to keep accounts of everything I hear and see. I interviewed people, before the Scientists locked me up. Despite my 'crimes', I consider myself a Generation A historian. I want to get down everything that happened – the protests, the Towers, the riots and battles – that led to me – to all of us – being up here.

And what being up here really means.

And the things I've heard, and imagined of what it is like to be out there, now.

Is it as desolate as the Scientists tell us? Is it just one big puddle of murk? If you can exist out there, why do they say we can't?

The facts are being washed away, like the cities and towns destroyed by the rain and then the waves that came, stopped and then kept coming, some ten years ago now. I get the feeling I am being eradicated too. There is a step-by-step approach to my non-existence, happening just outside the door to my quarters. With no way of measuring, I can't tell if my portion sizes are shrinking, but my stomach tells me that they are. My illness does not worsen, but neither does it improve. I stagnate here. I sit still, and long for wings.

I wish I could hand you something out of the window, but it won't open. It is a shame, I was always partial to a crisp apple when I write, curling up tighter with every crunch, but maybe you are too young to know what an apple is.

They used to grow on trees. Their leaves, even when new, were a lush green. There were many different types, but they had blossom in common, able to withstand the fiercest gust.

A bit like you.

I had forgotten about apple blossom. I must write that down.

Dear Architects

Dear Architects,

Good effort. You bet on the future, and it paid off. You didn't enjoy the money, nor the fame, that you thought you would, but you were safe, and you got to live in me for a bit. But then you left in that Exodus, early on in my existence – you didn't like it here. I have to say that stung a bit, but I've had long enough to mull it over and I think I get it.

You lived to see me achieved. I understand – it took enough time. There were some months where my windows and cladding went up in minutes, and then a long, lazy summer where I sat open to the elements, no one believing I was worth anything. A sunny, hot summer. I can still feel the burn. Can you?

Everyone was sure that things were changing for the better. Then came that sudden panic as it all got too warm and wet, and boy, did I start to go up quickly. Thousands of workers crawled about me, their yellow hard hats slick with the mist that had started to coil around my form. Some of them died in saving the world, falling at my feet, miles down in the soil.

Then there were the fires, lit by the anger of those left on the Outside.

The fires couldn't hurt me. In your sterling selection of steel – you saw to that.

When your bodies were found, drowned, after the Wave, they buried you down there too. They didn't have to look too hard to find your soggy, bloated forms. The water carried you back to me.

So, you lie at my base, in a specially designed, watertight (a bit late for that, perhaps) mausoleum that has space for your daughter too. The little girl you left behind, a Generation B – is all grown up. The child that you created, just as you created me. Is it pleasing to know she'll be buried in the earth, and not cremated like the others that live within me? That one day, you'll be reunited again?

It is significant that you lie so many generations down, it gives us all some perspective. The storeys of me are like the rings in a tree's trunk. Generations live within, each with their own understanding of how they came to be.

I may have had a false start or two, but I think it has turned out for the best. Inside me, people are alive – more than alive. They're doing what humans do – eating, crying, laughing, even procreating! The Scientists harped on about altitude and shock and fertility, and now we've got a Generation C on its way! Who knows, maybe we'll have even more family members to bury alongside you, one day. Grandchildren, great-nephews.

You'll be someone's ancestors.

We are, of course, quite 'space-poor'. And the yellow and blue sectors aren't getting any younger, are they? It is for the Scientists to decide who goes, and when. Up here, tough decisions will have to be made.

The Greenhouse is as gloriously abundant as you'd both always hoped. There are still one or two weaker entrances, allowing the occasional contraband magic to occur. Yes, there are people who survived the Waves. I would like to know why they survived, whether their motivation to live on went beyond existence, if it was fuelled by whatever fuelled you, on the momentous day that you drew me up on a paper napkin, on a ferry back from your island.

Still, as I said, *good effort*, my dear Architects. For as long as I stand (and thanks to you, it'll be a good long while), I'll remember your kindness at thinking me into existence.

The lives I carry inside, if they thought about it for more than a moment, might be grateful to you, too.

Then again, asking a human for that sort of perspective is like asking steel to feel emotion.

Am I right?